I0620715

Peter Pan:
Welcome to My Nightmare

By

Will Savive

DelGrande Publishing
Long Island, NY
Copyright © 2024 Will Savive/DelGrande
Publishing

ISBN: 978-1-7374865-9-6
ASIN: B0DLV9BRN2

Author's Website:

https://willsavive.com/

Peter Pan

**To get all the latest news on horror
movies & books, join:**

https://www.facebook.com/WillSavive

ISBN-13: 978-1-7374865-9-6
BISAC: Psychological Horror

Printed in the United States of America

Praise for
Sloan Parker's Other Books

"Sloan Parker is an amazing writer. Her work is beautiful and touching and emotional. If you haven't read any of her books, I suggest you run out and do so!"

—Sadonna at The Armchair Reader

"...I have loved every one of Sloan Parker's books and this one is no different. ...exciting, suspenseful and most importantly, romantic. The love story between Walter and Kevin is so sweet and real. They have a connection that can't be denied by either one of them."

—Literary Nook on HOW TO SAVE A LIFE

"...a smoothly flowing plot that has enough angst, obstacles, and mystery to keep you glued from the first page to the last... I thoroughly enjoyed reading this fascinating and enthralling book and would definitely recommend it to anyone looking for a fantastic read that is worth every minute spent on it."

— Trish at Mrs. Condit Reads Books on HOW TO SAVE A LIFE

"...a beautiful love story... You can't help but fall in love with Linc and Jay. I can't recommend it enough. I can't wait to read more books by this author."

—Caroline at Book Lovers Inc. on BREATHE

"...an incredibly poignant story where the emotions are profoundly moving, the characterization is perfect, and the suspense is riveting."

— Nannette at Joyfully Reviewed on BREATHE

"...an emotional and sensual blockbuster."

—Joyfully Reviewed on MORE

OTHER TITLES BY SLOAN PARKER

More (More Book 1)
More Than Most (More Book 2)
How to Save a Life (The Haven Book 1)
Breathe
Take Me Home
More Than Just a Good Book
I Swear to You

Chapter 1

The Dance

In the dimly lit office of the mental institution, the air hung heavy with the scent of old books and polished wood. The walls, lined with diplomas and framed certificates, seemed to whisper the weight of authority and knowledge. A large mahogany desk dominated the room, its surface cluttered with patient files, a steaming cup of coffee, and a potted plant that looked as if it had seen better days.

Seated behind the desk was *Dr. Eleanor Hart*, the head administrator, her expression a blend of concern and professionalism. Her dark hair was pulled back into a tight bun, and her spectacles perched on the edge of her nose as she scrutinized a file. Across from her sat *Dr. Mark Sullivan*, a psychologist with a furrowed brow, fidgeting with the sleeves of his lab coat.

"Eleanor," he began, his voice steady but tinged with urgency, "I've been reviewing the patient's case file, and I have determined that he has severe paranoid delusions."

Dr. Hart looked up, her green eyes narrowing slightly as she looked up at him from the file in her hand.

"Yes, that's what I called you in here to discuss. What's your assessment?"

Dr. Sullivan leaned forward, his hands clasped tightly.

"His delusions of grandeur are alarming. He not only believes he possesses extraordinary abilities, but he also exhibits signs of severe psychotic episodes. During the last session, he claimed he could fly and insisted that others were conspiring to silence him."

Eleanor nodded, her fingers tapping rhythmically on the desk.

"And how did he respond when you attempted to challenge those beliefs?"

"With a mix of anger and fear," he replied. "He became agitated, even hostile. It's as if his entire identity hinges on these delusions. I worry that confronting him directly might exacerbate his condition."

Dr. Hart sighed, glancing out the window where the autumn leaves danced in the breeze.

"We need to find a balance between treatment and validation. If we dismiss his feelings outright, we risk pushing him further into his psychosis. What do you suggest?"

Dr. Sullivan took a moment, contemplating.

"I propose a gradual approach. We could introduce cognitive-behavioral techniques, gently guiding him to recognize the discrepancy between his beliefs and reality. Perhaps group therapy could help him see that he is not alone in his struggles."

"Group therapy?" Dr. Hart raised an eyebrow, intrigued. "You think that would be effective?"

"Absolutely," he replied with conviction. "Hearing others share their experiences might help him feel less isolated. It could also provide a safe space for him to express himself without judgement."

Eleanor leaned back in her chair, considering his words.

"You're right. Isolation can be detrimental. We'll need to monitor him closely, though. If he senses any threat to his delusions, we could be facing a crisis. I fear that the patient could be very dangerous."

Dr. Sullivan nodded, a flicker of resolve in his eyes.

"I agree. I'll prepare the group session framework and start working with him on the cognitive techniques. I have a feeling there's more to his story than just the delusions."

As the two professionals continued to discuss strategies, the weight of their responsibility hung palpably in the air. Outside, the world continued to turn, blissfully unaware of the battles being fought within the walls of the institution. Dr. Hart and Dr. Sullivan were determined to navigate the murky waters of the mind, seeking to bring light to the shadows that plagued their patient's reality while also trying to keep the facility safe.

My Darling

In the quiet, moonlit corner of London, a gentle breeze swept through the open second floor window of the *Darling* household. From his perch just outside the residence, *Peter Pan* had often watched Wendy Darling through her window, captivated by her vivacious spirit and the stories she wove for her brothers. But tonight was different. As he floated in the cool night air, his heart sank at the sight unfolding within the room. Wendy's parents were there, their voices sharp and angry, cutting through the night like a bitter wind. Peter's small frame pressed against the glass as he witnessed the chaos, each shout sending a shiver down his spine. He felt an overwhelming urge to intervene, to swoop in and rescue her from the harshness of reality, yet he hesitated, feeling helpless as he observed the turmoil.

When the door slammed shut and silence fell, the oppressive weight of the moment lingered. Wendy's two younger brothers, faces pale and eyes wide, retreated to their beds, leaving Wendy behind in the dim light of her room. She sat at the edge of her bed, her shoulders trembling as tears glistened like stars in her eyes. Peter's heart ached for her; he could see the strength in her spirit, yet it was overshadowed by the pain she had just endured. He knew he couldn't just stand by any longer. A fire ignited within him, pushing him to summon the courage he had always possessed in the face of danger, but now called for something far more delicate.

Peter moved resolutely toward the window, his flight purposeful, his pulse quickening.

"Wendy," he called softly, his voice barely above a whisper, yet it held a warmth that cut through the darkness of her sorrow. Startled, she looked up, her tear-streaked face illuminated by the moonlight. In that moment, as their eyes locked, Peter felt an unspoken promise pass between them. He stepped through the window, crossing the threshold into her world, ready to offer her the comfort and adventure she so deserved. "It's okay," he said gently, his voice filled with sincerity.

"I'm here now. You're not alone."

As Peter found his bearings, the air seemed charged with a blend of vulnerability and hope. He noticed the small details that made her space uniquely hers: the meticulously arranged stuffed toys lined up on the shelf, the colorful drawings pinned to the walls, and the books stacked high beside her bed. Each item told a story of her imagination and resilience. In particular, he noticed a drawing hanging on the wall of a place that looked a lot like the place where he resided, *Neverland*. He knew then that Wendy longed for something more than her current life had to offer. Despite the recent chaos, there was a certain magic in the room, an echo of dreams waiting to be fulfilled. Wendy blinked at him in disbelief, her tears momentarily forgotten as her mind struggled to comprehend the presence of this mesmerizing young boy standing before her.

"Who... who are you?" she finally managed to ask, her voice trembling but curious. There was a spark in her eyes, a glimmer of the adventurous spirit that Peter admired so much.

"I'm *Peter Pan*," he replied, a hint of pride in his tone. "I've watched you tell stories, and I've always wanted to meet the girl who creates such wonderful worlds. If you come away with me, you will never look so sad as you do now." Wendy turned to him, her eyes filled with unshed tears.

"It's my parents," she admitted, her voice trembling. "They fight all the time. It's like I'm invisible… or worse, the reason for their anger." She glanced toward the door, half-expecting it to burst open with another round of shouting. He took a step closer, his heart swelling with purpose.

"You shouldn't have to face all this alone. I can show you a place where the skies are endless, where dreams come alive, and where no one will ever hurt you again." Wendy's initial surprise began to transform into a flicker of hope.

"A place like where?" she whispered, her imagination igniting at the mention of magical lands she had only read about in books. Peter nodded vigorously, his eyes gleaming with mischief and excitement.

"A magical place called *Neverland*!

We can fly away, just you and me. You can be the brave leader of our adventures, and together we can escape the shadows of this place." As he spoke, Wendy felt a connection blossoming between them—an understanding that transcended the pain of her reality. For the first time in what felt like forever, she began to believe in the possibility of freedom and joy, and the idea of embarking on an adventure with Peter lit a fire in her heart that she thought had long been extinguished.

Wendy's heart was filled with excitement at the thought of leaving her troubles behind. The idea of flying away with Peter filled her with both excitement and apprehension; she had always dreamed of adventures beyond the confines of her room, yet the weight of her parents' anger still lingered in her mind.

Suddenly, a soft tinkling sound interrupted their exchange, like tiny bells ringing on a gentle breeze. Without warning, a small beam of light zipped into the room, her wings shimmering with an iridescent glow. The strange ball of light hovered near Peter, her expression a combination of mischief and jealousy, casting a sharp glance at Wendy.

Wendy, taken aback by the unexpected arrival, blinked in astonishment.

"What is that strand of flying light?" she asked, her voice fused with awe and confusion. Peter grinned, his eyes sparkling with the thrill of introducing his fairy friend.

"This is *Tinkerbell*," he said, beaming with pride. "She's my fairy companion." As Wendy reached out tentatively to touch Tinkerbell's luminescent form, Tink shot her hand away with an indignant flick of her wrist, her wings fluttering in agitation. Wendy recoiled, surprised by the fairy's sudden aggression, the warmth of her curiosity quickly replaced by a chill of uncertainty.

Tinkerbell flitted closer to Peter, her tiny voice rising in a flurry of unintelligible sounds that only Peter could understand, clearly voicing her discontent about Wendy's presence.

"What's she saying?" Wendy asked, intrigued yet slightly intimidated. Peter chuckled softly, his brow furrowing in concentration as he translated Tink's spirited protest.

"She doesn't like the idea of you coming to Neverland," he said, a hint of protest in his tone. A playful argument ensued as Peter defended Wendy, insisting that she would bring joy and wonder to their adventures, while Tink crossed her arms, her wings drooping in defiance. The air was thick with tension, yet a spark of excitement lingered, hinting at the adventures that lay ahead in their enchanted realm.

As the playful argument between Peter and Tinkerbell continued, the atmosphere in the room shifted, charged with the energy of their whimsical banter. Peter leaned closer to Tink, his eyes dancing with laughter.

"Come on, Tink! You know she'd love it there. Imagine all the stories she could tell!" he urged, gesturing animatedly. Tinkerbell, however, was not easily swayed. With a huff, she darted to the window, hovering near the moonlight, her wings glinting like shards of glass. "You're just jealous, Tink!" Peter teased, a wide smile spreading across his face. "There's enough room in Neverland for both of you."

Wendy watched the exchange, a surge of adrenaline rushing through her. She had always dreamt of visiting a place like Neverland, but she feared the effect it might have on Peter's relationship with Tinkerbell.

"I didn't mean to intrude," Wendy said gently, her voice tinged with sincerity. "I only want to experience the magic you've described." Tinkerbell turned to Wendy, her eyes narrowing in suspicion, but Peter quickly intervened.

"See, Tink? She understands! She's not here to take me away from you. We can all have fun together!" His enthusiasm was contagious, yet Tink remained skeptical, crossing her tiny arms defiantly. Wendy hesitated for a few moments, her thoughts tumbling over one another.

"But... my parents?"

"Your parents?" Peter interrupted, his expression shifting to one of concern. "Do they make you happy?" Wendy sighed, a lump forming in her throat.

"Not really," she replied. Peter

stepped closer, his voice gentle yet insistent.

"In Neverland, you'll be seen and heard. You'll have adventures beyond your wildest dreams. No one will tell you what to do, and you can fly!"

"Fly? Like a bird?" she gasped, her heart racing at the thought. Peter nodded energetically, his laughter ringing like music in the air.

"Yes! All it takes is a sprinkle of fairy dust, a little bit of faith, and most importantly, you must think happy thoughts. It's the most exhilarating feeling in the world, soaring through the clouds and dancing with the stars!" Wendy's eyes sparkled with a mix of shock and wonder.

"But how? I can't just... fly!" she stammered, nearly breathless with excitement. Peter grinned and reached into his pocket, pulling out a small vial of shimmering dust.

"Tinkerbell's special fairy dust! Just a sprinkle will do," he explained, holding it up like a precious treasure. "Trust me, Wendy! You just have to believe in the magic." With a hesitant smile, Wendy nodded, feeling a rush of courage. As Peter sprinkled the twinkling dust over her, a warm sensation enveloped her, and she felt an incredible lightness as if her feet were lifting off the ground. "Now, let go of your fears and let your imagination take flight!" he encouraged, and with a sudden burst of joy, Wendy found herself rising into the air, her laughter blending with the wind as she hovered alongside Peter. As Wendy floated in mid-air, her pulse quickened with exhilaration and disbelief.

"I can't believe it! I'm really flying!" she shouted, her voice a blend of joy and astonishment as she floated around the room. Peter laughed, his laughter resonated like a melodious tune.

"Told you! Just feel the magic, Wendy! It's all around us!" He twirled in the air, performing playful loops and flips, encouraging her to join in on the fun. Wendy, still in awe, attempted a clumsy spin, her laughter bubbling over as she realized how free and weightless she felt. Suddenly, Wendy's expression grew somber, and she sank to the floor. Peter followed.

"What's wrong, Wendy?" he asked in confusion.

"But what about my brothers?" she cried. "I can't leave them behind."

"Bring them!" Peter beamed. "They'll love it too. We'll all have fun together, fighting pirates and playing with the *Lost Boys*. It'll be just like a storybook come to life!"

Wendy's heart fluttered at the idea. She imagined herself soaring through the sky, the wind whipping through her hair, leaving behind the suffocating confines of her home.

"It sounds wonderful, Peter, but what if... what if it's not real?"

Peter grinned, a glimmer of mischief in his eyes.

"What's real, anyway? Sometimes, you have to leap into the unknown to find out. You deserve to be happy, Wendy. You deserve to be free." Tears brimmed in her eyes as she contemplated his words.

"But what if I get lost? I've never been on my own before." Peter took her hand, his grip warm and reassuring.

"You won't be alone. I'll be with you

every step of the way. We'll make memories that'll last forever. And if you ever feel scared, just remember, you can always fly back home." Wendy looked out the window again, the stars shining brighter than ever.

"I want to believe you, Peter. I really do. But it's such a big decision..."

"Sometimes the biggest decisions lead to the best adventures," he said softly. "You have the chance to choose your own path. Why not choose the one that sets you free?" With a deep breath, Wendy closed her eyes, envisioning the life she longed for, a life filled with laughter, adventure, and magic.

"Okay, Peter. I'll go with you," she said with excitement. Tinkerbell let out an exasperated sigh, her tiny arms crossed tightly as she turned her head away, a look of disdain etched across her delicate features.

At that moment, as Wendy wrapped up her thought, her brothers, *John*—the middle child—and *Michael*—the youngest—began to stir, slowly rising from their beds with sleepy expressions. As John and

Michael rubbed the sleep from their eyes, they were greeted by the sight of their sister, Wendy, animatedly conversing with a boy who appeared to be made of pure mischief and magic. The room was bathed in a soft glow from the fairy dust that lingered in the air, and the boy's laughter danced like music around them.

"Wendy?" John called out, his voice still thick with slumber. "Who's this?" Wendy turned, her eyes sparkling with enthusiasm.

"It's Peter Pan! He's invited us to fly to Neverland!" The boys exchanged bewildered glances, their minds struggling to grasp the reality of the situation.

"Fly? To Neverland?" Michael echoed, his voice a mix of disbelief and wonder. "Is that even possible?" Wendy nodded eagerly, her cheeks flushed with exhilaration.

"Yes! Peter says we can all fly together! Just imagine the adventures we could have!" Peter stepped forward, a grin spreading across his face.

"Trust me, it's as easy as dreaming! All you need is a sprinkle of fairy dust." With that, he produced the shimmering vial, and in a swift motion, he sprinkled the glowing dust over John and Michael. The moment it touched their skin, they felt a warmth spreading through them, lifting their spirits as if they were already soaring into the sky.

With a whoop of joy, Peter took to the air, followed closely by Wendy, John, and Michael, who were soon swept up in the thrill of flight. The room transformed into a whirlwind of laughter and amazement as they zipped around, their hearts racing with the exhilaration of defying gravity.

"Look at us! We're flying!" John shouted, his voice filled with pure delight as he spun in mid-air. Michael clapped his hands, giggling uncontrollably as he floated beside his sister.

"This is incredible!" Wendy exclaimed, her joy infectious. The four of them flew in circles, reveling in their newfound freedom, before Peter pointed toward the open window, a shimmer of adventure in his eyes.

"Are you ready to go to Neverland, have wild adventures, tell amazing stories, and never ever grow old?" With a collective cheer, they soared through the window, leaving behind the ordinary world and embracing the magic that awaited them in the mysterious land of dreams.

Chapter 2

Welcome to Neverland

On a sunny afternoon, The *Jolly Roger* lay majestically anchored close to the sandy shore, its black sails billowing softly in the gentle breeze like the wings of a great raven. The ship's hull, a dark silhouette against the vibrant rays of the sun, was adorned with intricate carvings of mythical sea creatures, their eyes seemingly glinting with mischief. Cannons peeked from portholes, ready to defend against any unwelcome intruders, while the skull and crossbones flag fluttered high above, a stark warning to all who dared approach. The sound of the waves lapping against the sturdy timbers created a rhythmic lullaby, harmonizing with the distant calls of seabirds circling overhead.

On deck, the crew of ruffians and scallywags busied themselves with their routines, snappy banter, and shouts mingling with the salty air. The ship's deck was strewn with treasures: glittering gold doubloons and mysterious trinkets collected from countless adventures. The scent of fresh sea air mingled with the faint aroma of cooking, wafting from the galley below deck. However, as the sun climbed higher, casting a golden hue over the ship, *Captain Hook* was not concerned with the treasures that awaited him and the adventures that lay just beyond the horizon; his mind was obsessed with only one thing: catching the elusive Peter Pan.

Captain Hook leaned back in his lavishly decorated office below deck, surrounded by the glimmering treasures of his pirate conquests. The mahogany desk was strewn with maps marked in red, each one detailing various routes through Neverland and the mysterious hideouts of the infamous Peter Pan. The air was heavy with the scent of salt and the faint echoes of waves crashing against the hull, creating a backdrop for Hook's dark thoughts.

As Captain Hook reclined in his carved mahogany chair, the dim glow of lantern light flickered across his quarters, illuminating the intricate details of his lucky *amulet*—a small, oval-shaped charm made from a deep, iridescent stone encased in twisted silver filigree. The amulet was a family heirloom, passed down through generations of Hook men, each having sworn that it held the key to fortune and success. On this day it felt unusually warm in his palm, almost vibrating with energy as he turned it over, tracing the patterns etched into its surface. With every glance at the amulet, his mind raced with schemes to ensnare Peter Pan, the boy who had eluded him for so long. Hook's heart thrummed with desperation and determination, convinced that the amulet would turn his misfortunes into triumph, guiding his hand as he plotted to finally capture the evasive sprite and reclaim his lost honor.

Smee, his loyal right-hand man, stood beside him, an imposing figure with broad shoulders and a beard that seemed to hide half his face. His eyes, however, sparkled with a mix of admiration and confusion as he watched Hook rise and pace back and forth.

"Captain, you've been at this for

hours! Perhaps we should take a break?" Smee suggested, scratching his head.

"Nonsense, Smee!" Hook snapped, his voice sharp as a dagger. "That wretched boy has eluded me for far too long. I will not rest until Peter Pan is captured and brought to his end. Imagine the glory! The tales they'll tell of Captain Hook, the man who finally defeated the boy who never grew up!"

He paused, his fingers drumming on the desk, then turned sharply to Smee. "We need to know where Peter's hidden lair lies—the very heart of his domain! The *Lost Boys* will know, and I have just the pawn to extract that information."

With a flourish, Hook strode over to a large chest in the corner of the office. The chest creaked ominously as he opened it, revealing a battered and bruised Lost Boy named *Harry*, who was tied up and gagged. His wild hair was matted, and his eyes glinted with defiance despite the circumstances.

"Look at him, Smee," Hook said, a sly smile creeping onto his face. "A perfect specimen of resilience. But resilience can be broken. We'll see just how tough he is when I apply a little pressure."

Smee looked uncertain, shifting his weight from one foot to the other.

"Are you sure that's wise, Captain? The boy looks like he's been through enough already."

"Wise? Oh, Smee, what do I care for wisdom when revenge is at hand?" Hook replied, his voice rising with excitement. He leaned closer to the boy, narrowing his eyes. "You listen well, lad! I have a simple question, and your life depends on how well you answer it. Where does Peter Pan sleep? Where can I find him?"

The boy's eyes widened in fear, and he shook his head vigorously, the gag muffling his protests. Hook's smile faded, replaced by a scowl.

"Very well," Hook said coldly. "If you wish to play the hero, prepare to face the consequences." He gestured to Smee, who stepped forward, a hint of reluctance in his eyes.

"But Captain—"

"Silence!" Hook barked. "We do not have time for your hesitations. Let's begin the interrogation." As Smee reached for the boy, Hook's thoughts spun with visions of victory. He could almost hear the cheers of his crew, the tales of his conquest echoing across the seas. All he needed was a clue, and then he would finally have the upper hand over Peter Pan.

"Now, let's get started, shall we?" Hook said, his voice dripping with malice as the shadows of the room deepened around them. With a flick of his wrist, Captain Hook motioned for Smee to tighten the ropes around Harry's wrists, ensuring further discomfort. The boy squirmed, eyes wide with terror as he realized the gravity of his situation.

"Don't be foolish! You're only making things worse for yourself," Hook taunted, leaning closer, allowing his menacing presence to loom over the chest. "I can assure you, I have methods that will make you wish you had spoken sooner."

The boy continued to shake his head defiantly, his spirit unyielding despite his battered state. Hook admired that spirit, but it only fueled his anger further. He turned to Smee, who was watching nervously, and snapped, "Bring me the tools from the galley!"

Smee hesitated for a moment, glancing at the captive boy with a mixture of pity and fear.

"But Captain, do we really need to resort to—"

"Do as I command, Smee!" Hook interrupted, his voice echoing through the small office like a clap of thunder. Smee shuffled off to fetch the requested items, leaving Hook alone with the boy.

"Now, let's have a chat, shall we?" Hook said, straightening up and adjusting his hat. "You may think you're a brave little warrior, but bravery will only get you so far. I can make your life a living nightmare, or I can make it... slightly more pleasant. You have one chance. Choose wisely."

The boy's gaze flickered to Hook's face, a blend of fear and anger etched into his features. Hook continued, "Tell me Peter's hiding place, and I promise you'll be treated with a modicum of respect. I might even let you keep your precious life."

The boy's brow furrowed, and he seemed to weigh his options. Hook could see the conflict within him, a battle between loyalty to Peter and the instinct for survival.

Moments later, Smee returned, carrying a small collection of kitchen utensils—a rolling pin, a couple of sharp knives, and a large wooden spoon. Hook's eyes gleamed with delight at the sight of the tools, an assortment that could turn the interrogation into a theatrical production.

"Excellent, Smee! Now, let's see how long he can hold out," Hook said, brandishing the rolling pin like a sword.

With a dramatic flourish, Hook raised the pin to the boy's face, who recoiled instinctively. "You see, lad, it's all a game of persuasion. You can either tell me what I want to know, or I can make this... rather unpleasant."

The boy's resolve began to crack, his breath quickening as he glanced at the tools before him.

"I... I won't tell you anything!" he managed to say through the loose gag, his voice muffled but resolute.

"Ah, the spirit of youth!" Hook mocked, lowering the rolling pin. "But remember, every hero has a breaking point. I'll give you a moment to reconsider while I prepare my methods." As Hook turned away for a brief moment, Smee stepped closer to the boy, his expression softening.

"Look, mate, you really don't want to go through with this. The captain can be... well, he's not exactly known for his kindness."

The boy shot Smee a glare, but the flicker of uncertainty in his eyes was evident. He breathed heavily, his thoughts racing. He knew he had to stay strong for Peter and the other Lost Boys, but the fear of the looming threat was palpable.

"Enough of this chit-chat!" Hook shouted, spinning around again. "Time to play! You can start by telling me where Peter Pan's living quarters are—an easy task for a boy who wants to keep his skin intact!"

As the tension in the room escalated, the boy's heart raced. He knew he had to think fast. With a surge of courage, he finally resolved to protect Peter at all costs.

"You'll never find him!" he shouted defiantly, his voice breaking free from the gag, even if just for a moment.

Hook's eyes narrowed, a dark smile spreading across his face.

"Very well, then. I hope you're ready for what's coming next."

Just as Captain Hook leaned closer to the captive Lost Boy, the atmosphere charged with tension and anticipation, the door swung open with a loud crash. A crew member burst in, his face pale and eyes wide with urgency.

"Captain! Sir!" the crewman gasped, breathless from running. "You need to see this!"

Hook's eyes flared with fury, his expression darkening as he turned sharply towards the intruder.

"What is the meaning of this interruption?" he thundered, the rolling pin hovering dangerously close to the boy's face. "I was in the midst of a most important inquiry!" The crewman faltered, the sight of Hook's fury making him momentarily tremble.

"I... I apologize, Captain, but it's urgent! I was using the telescope, and I saw Peter Pan!" Hook's irritation shifted to intrigue, a fire igniting in his eyes.

"What did you say?" he demanded, leaning closer, his previous intentions forgotten as he focused entirely on the crewman. The boy tied up in the chest felt a moment of relief and a surge of emotion as he realized that perhaps fate had intervened in his favor.

"Peter Pan and a few of the Lost Boys are flying high in the sky, headed east!" the crewman exclaimed, his voice breaking slightly with excitement.

"East, you say?" Hook repeated, a smile creeping across his face, transforming his fury into exhilaration. "Do you mean to tell me they are flying right above us?"

"Aye, Captain! I swear it!" the crewman affirmed, his enthusiasm growing. "They were soaring just above the treetops, laughing and playing as they always do. We must act quickly!" Hook's mind raced, visions of finally capturing Peter Pan flooding his thoughts.

"Smee!" he bellowed, spinning toward his first mate, who had been anxiously waiting in the corner. "Prepare the row boats, and ready the crew to set sail immediately!" Smee jumped to attention and quickly headed above deck.

"Aye, Captain! Right away!" He rushed out of the office, shouting orders to the crew as Hook turned his attention back to the crewman.

"Why didn't you come in sooner?" Hook chastised, trying to suppress his excitement. "A moment wasted can cost us dearly!"

"I-I thought it best to confirm what I saw before disturbing you, sir," the crewman stammered, his voice steadying as he saw Hook's anger dissipate. "I didn't want to interrupt your... business."

"Business? Ha!" Hook laughed, the sound rich and dark. "You've done well, my friend. This could be the very opportunity we've been waiting for!" The boy in the chest watched in disbelief as the pirate captain's demeanor shifted so quickly, the terror of the interrogation fading into the background.

"Gather the crew!" Hook called, his voice booming with authority. "We shall follow that boy and capture him once and for all! No more games, no more delays! We will not let him slip through our fingers this time!"

"Charting the course, Captain!" Smee shouted from outside, his voice echoing as he rallied the crew. With renewed energy, Hook turned back to the Lost Boy, a wicked grin on his face. "Consider yourself fortunate, lad. You've been spared for now. But don't think I've forgotten you. Once we've dealt with Peter Pan, we shall return to our little game." The boy's heart sank as he realized that the reprieve was only temporary, but perhaps there was still hope. If Peter was out there, he would fight for them all.

As Hook strode out of the office, his crew bustling around him, he felt a surge of anticipation course through him.

"To the row boats, now! Let's catch that little pest!" he shouted, the thrill of the chase igniting the hearts of his crew.

And as Hook's men rowed furiously, cutting through the waves towards the eastern horizon, Harry remained trapped in the chest, the weight of the moment heavy on his shoulders. He knew Peter would need to be ready for whatever was coming, for Hook was determined, and the hunt was on.

As they approached the shore, the crew bustled with newfound energy, their shouts and laughter filling the air as they prepared for the chase. Hook stood at the helm, his eyes scanning the horizon, filled with anticipation and a hunger for revenge.

"Faster, you scallywags!" he bellowed, his voice booming over the sound of waves crashing against the side of the small boats. "We must catch them before they reach the safety of the trees!" The promise of capturing Peter Pan electrified the atmosphere, their spirits soaring as high as the lost boys they pursued.

Life's A Beach

The soft, powdery sand of Neverland crunched beneath their feet as Peter Pan, Tinkerbell, Wendy, John, and Michael stepped onto the sunlit shore. The vibrant turquoise waves rolled gently against the shoreline, and the air was alive with the sweet scent of blooming flowers mixed with salt. The towering palm trees swayed gracefully, their fronds creating a natural canopy that promised shelter.

"Look at this place!" John exclaimed, his eyes wide with wonder as he spun around, taking in the breathtaking beauty. "It's like nothing I've ever seen before!"

"I can't believe we're really here," Wendy said, her voice filled with awe. She knelt down to touch the sand, letting it slip through her fingers. "It feels like a dream."

"Not a dream, Wendy! It's real!" Peter laughed, soaring into the air with a playful twirl. "And it's just the beginning!"

Tinkerbell zipped around, her tiny wings shimmering in the sunlight, leaving a trail of pixie dust in her wake.

"Come on! There's so much to explore!" she chimed, her voice like tinkling bells. Peter hovered above a cluster of large, vibrant fruits hanging from a nearby tree.

"Wait right here!" he called down, darting effortlessly toward the branches. He plucked a glowing, exotic fruit that looked like a cross between a mango and a star, its colors shifting in the sunlight. With a triumphant grin, he flew back to the group.

"Look what I found!"

"What is it?" Michael asked, his eyes round with curiosity.

"Only one way to find out!" Peter said, taking a hearty bite. The juice dripped down his chin, and he smiled broadly. "Delicious!" Wendy took a bite next, her eyes lighting up.

"Oh, it's sweet and tangy! I've never tasted anything like it!" John, not wanting to be left out, grabbed one for himself and joined in.

"This is amazing! We have to find more!" Michael followed suit, his laughter ringing out as he joined his siblings in the delightful feast. With their spirits high and laughter in the air, they ventured deeper into the woods, their feet dancing over the dappled sunlight filtering through the trees. Tinkerbell darted between them, sprinkling pixie dust and urging them to run faster.

"Race you to that grove!" Peter shouted, his eyes sparkling with mischief.

"Wait for me!" Wendy called, her laughter mingling with the rustling leaves as she sprinted after him, her brothers close behind.

As they reached a clearing, Peter and Tinkerbell floated above them, basking in the joy of the moment.

"You know," Tinkerbell began, her voice laced with a hint of embarrassment, "Wendy does seem nice," Tink said reluctantly.

Peter grinned at her. "Oh, I know... I told you," he boasted. "She will fit in just right here among us."

Wendy watched them, a smile on her face, until Peter turned to her, inviting her to step away for a moment. They walked a little distance from the others, the sound of laughter fading into the background.

"Wendy," Peter said, his tone suddenly more serious, "what do you think of Neverland?" Wendy sighed, her gaze drifting toward the horizon where the ocean met the sky.

"It's like a dream come true. I feel like I could stay here forever." Peter chuckled, a playful glint in his eyes.

"Then let's just make sure you don't wake up!" Wendy smiled, her heart fluttering at his charm.

"So, what's next?" Wendy asked

curiously. Peter's expression brightened.

"We're going to fly to my home! It's where I live with the Lost Boys. You'll be like a mom to them. They'll love you!"

"Mom?" Wendy raised an eyebrow, intrigued yet amused. "But I'm just a girl!"

"Exactly! They need a mother. They need someone to keep them in line. Trust me, it'll be fun!" Peter replied with a wink.

Just then, Tinkerbell zipped back to them, her expression suddenly serious.

"Peter! I spotted several of Captain Hook's men coming ashore in rowboats!" Peter's smile vanished, replaced by a fierce determination.

"Hook! That old codfish is obsessed with me," he said, his voice low. "He wants me dead." Wendy's eyes widened, concern washing across her face.

"Who wants you dead," she asked nervously.

"This old pirate who once captured us and tried to enslave us," Peter says with a gleam in his eyes. "But we fought back, and Hook attacked me. So, I cut off his hand in battle, and we escaped. Now he wears a hook for a hand. He never quite forgave me for that."

"Oh, dear," Wendy cried. "What do we do?"

"Back to the hideout!" Peter commanded, taking her hand. "We can't let them find us. Follow me!"

As they dashed through the underbrush, the thrill of adventure surged within them, blending with the looming danger. The spirit of Neverland pulsed around them, promising magic and excitement, even as shadows lurked in the distance.

****

The oars of the rowboats splashed rhythmically against the water as Captain Hook and his twelve best warriors and trackers maneuvered the vessel onto the sandy shore. Once his boat was on dry land, Hook leaped out commandingly, the sound of his boots sinking into the sand echoing like a war drum.

"Spread out! Search every inch of this beach!" he ordered, his voice cutting through the air.

The crew fanned out, eyes scanning the surroundings, the sound of the ocean fading behind them. They moved with purpose. Hook felt a jolt of energy. He could almost taste the victory that awaited him. As they ventured further inland, one of the pirates, a wiry man named *Mullins*, suddenly stopped, crouching low.

"Captain! Over here!" he shouted, holding something aloft. The group gathered around him, curious.

"What is it, you fool?" Hook snapped, but his irritation turned to interest as he saw the small piece of the strange, colorful fruit clutched in Mullins' hand. The remnants glistened with juice, their vibrant colors unmistakable.

"They were here, Sir!" Mullins exclaimed, excitement bubbling in his voice. "Just moments ago!" Hook stepped closer, his eyes narrowing as he examined the fruit.

"So, they've been feasting on this peculiar delicacy," he mused, a sly smile creeping across his face. "This means we're on the right track. They can't be far."

"Shall we follow their trail, Captain?" another pirate asked, his brow furrowed with eagerness.

"Of course!" Hook barked, his voice rising with fervor. "Press on! They shall leave traces behind that giveaway their direction and positions. I want them tonight! I want Peter Pan and his little friends in my grasp! No more games!"

The crew nodded, their resolve hardening as they began to move deeper into the woods, the scent of the strange fruit lingering in the air like a beacon. They navigated through the dense underbrush, the sounds of nature surrounding them, but their focus was unwavering.

"Keep your eyes peeled!" Hook commanded, his voice a harsh whisper as they tread carefully. "We must find their hideout before nightfall! Pan is clever, but he cannot hide forever. This is the chance we've been waiting for!"

As they ventured onward, the pirates' footsteps were muffled by the soft earth, but the tension in the air was palpable. Each man felt the thrill of the hunt, the promise of capturing their elusive foe igniting a fire in their hearts.

"Captain," Mullins said, glancing back

with a glimmer of hope, "if we can find him tonight, we'll finally put an end to this nonsense."

"Indeed," Hook replied, his voice low and menacing. "And I will show that boy what it means to cross Captain Hook. He thinks he can play with the likes of me, but I will have the last laugh!"

With renewed vigor, the pirates pressed through the trees, their eyes darting in all directions as the sun had begun its descent. The group was keen to catch even the smallest sign of Peter and his friends. They found traces of shimmering trails of pixie dust sparkling in the remaining sunlight, small pockets of footprints, and scattered belongings of the group. The night was rapidly approaching, but Hook's resolve blazed brighter than the setting sun. The hunt was on, and the thrill of the chase filled the air, weaving together the fates of both the hunter and the hunted.

Chapter 3

Home Sweet Home

Beneath the towering canopies of the ancient trees in Neverland's *Enchanted Forest*, the light of day began to wane, casting long shadows that danced playfully on the forest floor. The air was filled with the sweet scent of blooming flowers and damp earth, a magical atmosphere that welcomed Peter Pan, Tinkerbell, Wendy, and her brothers, John and Michael, as they approached the humongous tree that served as Peter's hideout.

The tree was magnificent, its gnarled roots twisting and curling above the ground, creating natural seating areas where the Lost Boys often gathered. As they drew near, a group of exuberant Lost Boys emerged from behind the thick brush, their eyes wide with curiosity.

"Peter! You're back!" *Tootles* shouted, rushing forward with unbridled excitement. "Who are your friends?" Peter grinned, his eyes sparkling with delight.

"These are my new friends from the other world! This is Wendy," he said, gesturing toward her, "and these are her brothers, John and Michael." The Lost Boys exchanged glances, their expressions a filled with wonder and awe.

"Wendy?" *Nibs* echoed, tilting his head as if trying to understand the name. "What's a Wendy?"

"She's a girl!" *Slightly* shouted, bouncing on his toes. "We haven't seen a girl in years!"

"Yeah! A real girl!" piped up *Curly*, his eyes gleaming with excitement. "What's she like?"

Wendy smiled, feeling a flutter of warmth in her heart as the boys surrounded her, their enthusiasm infectious.

"I'm just like you, really. I love adventures and stories," she said, her voice gentle and inviting. Before she could say more, several Lost Boys dashed off into the thicket, shouting, *"Come on! We have to tell everyone!"* Within moments, they returned, followed by a swarm of Lost Boys, their laughter echoing through the trees. As they gathered outside the tree, the total number of Lost Boys swelled to thirty, all fixated on Wendy with wide, eager eyes. They pushed forward, each one wanting to be the first to greet her. The atmosphere buzzed with excitement as they began calling her "Mother," a title that both flattered and surprised her.

Peter decided to show Wendy around their home, which they accessed through an underground passage. Peter Pan and the Lost Boys had fashioned their home from the very roots and earth that surrounded them, creating a cozy underground refuge that was both whimsical and enchanting. The tunnels twisted and turned, resembling the intricate patterns of a spider's web, with walls adorned in soft moss and bioluminescent fungi that cast a gentle glow. This secretive realm was alive with the sounds of laughter and the faint rustle of leaves above, creating a harmonious symphony that blended seamlessly with the natural world outside.

As Peter led Wendy deeper into their underground sanctuary, she marveled at the cleverness of the Lost Boys' handiwork. Each chamber was uniquely designed, filled with makeshift furniture crafted from tree branches and oversized leaves, all surprisingly comfortable. Colorful lanterns hung from the low ceilings, illuminating the lively paintings of adventures and dreams sketched by the boys on the walls. In one nook, a gathering area buzzed with excitement as the boys shared tales of their latest exploits, their animated voices echoing through the tunnels, while in another, a cozy sleeping area was adorned with plush beds made from fluffy moss and feathers. It was a world untouched by the troubles of adulthood, where imagination reigned supreme.

Wendy's heart swelled with a sense of belonging as she watched the camaraderie among the boys. They were a ragtag family, bound by their shared adventures and the freedom of childhood. Peter, with his passionate spirit, animatedly recounted an escapade involving mermaids and pirates, his gestures exaggerated and full of life. The boys erupted into laughter, their joy infectious as they hung on his every word. For Wendy, this underground haven felt like a dream come true—a sanctuary where the burdens of the outside world melted away, replaced by the magic of friendship and the promise of endless adventures. In this hidden abode, she realized, they were free to be whoever they wanted, living in a realm where their imaginations could soar unfettered, just like Peter himself. After a tour, they led Wendy back outside.

"Mother!" they chirped in unison, their voices a sweet chorus. "Will you play with us?" A wave of affection washed over her as she realized how much these boys had longed for a maternal figure.

"Of course! What would you like to do?" she asked, her voice filled with warmth.

"Let's dance!" shouted *Swervy*, his passion contagious. The group quickly formed a circle, and as the sun dipped lower in the sky, they began to twirl and leap, laughter ringing through the forest. Wendy joined in, her heart light as she spun around, the Lost Boys following her lead, their laughter echoing like music. For hours, they played games—tag, hide-and-seek, and even a makeshift version of duck-duck-goose that had everyone rolling with laughter. Some of the boys took turns showing Wendy their handmade toys crafted from twigs and leaves, eager to impress her with their creations.

"Look at this!" *Knuckles* exclaimed, holding up a wooden bird he had whittled from a branch. "I made it just for you, Mother!" Wendy beamed, her eyes shining with pride.

"It's beautiful! You're all so talented!" she praised, and the boy's face lit up at her approval. As the sun began to set, painting the sky in shades of orange and purple, Peter gathered everyone around a crackling fire that had been set up in a small clearing. The Lost Boys settled in, their faces aglow with the warmth of the flames, and they looked expectantly at Peter.

As the fire crackled softly, casting flickering shadows that danced across the faces of the gathered crew, Peter Pan leaned closer, his expression shifting from playful to serious. The Lost Boys, Wendy, John, and Michael settled in, their anticipation palpable. The air grew heavy with excitement, and Tinkerbell flitted nearby, her light dimming as she sensed the change in mood.

"Gather 'round, everyone," Peter said, his voice lowering to a conspiratorial whisper. "I'm about to tell you a story that will send shivers down your spine. This is the tale of the *Night Stalker*."

The boys leaned in, eyes wide, their bodies hummed with tension at the prospect of a spine-chilling story. Peter's voice dropped to a hushed tone, the atmosphere thickening with suspense.

"Lurking in the shadows of Neverland is a monstrous figure known as the *Night Stalker*. It is a creature that embodies the darkness within every child's heart. Its form shifts and writhes, a mass of shadows and despair, always watching, always waiting."

The fire crackled ominously as Peter spoke, and the Lost Boys shivered, glancing nervously at the darkened trees surrounding them. "It feeds on the dreams of the young, twisting them into nightmares, leaving its victims ensnared in fear. Have you ever felt that chill in the air when the sun sets? That's the Night Stalker drawing near."

"Ugh, stop it!" Tootles shouted, though his eyes betrayed his fear. "You're scaring us!"

"It's supposed to be scary!" Peter replied, grinning mischievously. "But listen closely, for it's not just a story. The Night Stalker is drawn to those who harbor doubts or insecurities. It whispers insidious thoughts, growing louder with each passing moment, until you can't tell what's real anymore." Wendy wrapped her arms around her knees, feeling a chill crawl up her spine.

"What happens if it finds you?" she asked, her voice barely above a whisper. Peter continued, his voice dropping even lower, wrapping them all in the depth of the tale.

"Its presence is felt in the deepest hours of the night when shadows stretch across the ground, and the air grows thick with dread. Those who encounter it often find themselves paralyzed by fear, unable to escape the clutches of their own imagination."

The Lost Boys gasped, some clutching each other as Peter's words painted vivid, terrifying images in their minds.

"And if you ever hear your name whispered in the dark... run. Run as fast as you can, for the Night Stalker has chosen you!"

The fire crackled louder, and a gust of wind rustled the leaves overhead, adding to the eerie atmosphere. The boys shifted uneasily, glancing around as if expecting the creature to emerge from the shadows.

"Peter, stop!" John said, trying to sound brave. "You're making it too real!" But Peter only chuckled darkly, enjoying the effect his story had on them.

"That's the fun of it, John! But don't worry, I'll protect you all. Just remember, the Night Stalker is not real... well, not unless you believe in it."

As the tension hung in the air, the Lost Boys began to chant, *"Wendy! Wendy! Tell us a story!"* Their voices filled the air, eager for something to lighten the mood. Wendy, sensing their need for comfort, smiled gently.

"Alright, alright. I'll tell you a story,

but it won't be scary like Peter's story. This one is about a beautiful moment back home." The boys settled back, their eyes still wide, but their hearts lightening as Wendy began.

"Once, during the summer, my family had a picnic in the park. The sun was shining, and the flowers were in bloom. We spread out a blanket, and my brothers and I played games while my mother prepared the food. There were sandwiches, fresh fruit, and a big jug of lemonade." As Wendy spoke, her voice warmed the air around them, creating a vivid picture. "We laughed and chased each other, and at one point, my father taught us how to fly kites. The sky was filled with colors as our kites danced in the wind, soaring high above us, just like Peter does here in Neverland."

The Lost Boys listened with rapt attention, their fear of the Night Stalker fading as they imagined the joyful scene. "And in that moment, I felt so happy. We were all together, sharing laughter and love, and I remember thinking that nothing could be better than that day." Wendy's story wrapped around them like a warm blanket, dispelling the remnants of fear that lingered from Peter's tale. The boys sighed contentedly, their imaginations now filled with images of sunny picnics instead of lurking shadows.

"See?" Peter said, grinning. "Happy stories can chase away the darkness just as easily as the light of day." As the stars began to twinkle above, Wendy finished her story, and the Lost Boys erupted into cheers, their spirits lifted. The laughter and joy returned, filling the night air with warmth and camaraderie.

"Thank you, Mother!" they exclaimed, their voices ringing through the trees. They felt safe and content, knowing that together, they could face anything— even the whispers of the Night Stalker lurking in the shadows.

Ambushed

As the campfire they had created crackled, popped, and sent sparks spiraling into the night sky, Captain Hook and his men, who were having a hard time tracking Peter, caught a glimpse of the fire from a distance. Far off in the dense underbrush, Captain Hook and his crew crouched low, their eyes fixed on the flickering light that betrayed the location of Peter and his friends. Hook's jaw tightened as he waved his hand to signal for silence.

"Steady now, lads," he whispered, a wicked smile curling his lips. "We've finally found them. Wait for my command." The pirates crept closer, moving like phantoms through the trees, their hearts racing with anticipation. Each step was calculated, every rustle of leaves silenced by Hook's commanding presence. They positioned themselves strategically around the camp, hiding behind bushes and trunks, their eyes gleaming with malice. Peter, filled with laughter, suddenly paused, a shiver racing down his spine. He sensed something was amiss.

"Do you hear that?" he asked, glancing around warily. The laughter faded, replaced by an unsettling silence that hung heavily in the air.

"Maybe it's just the wind," Michael suggested, though his voice trembled slightly. Wendy clutched her brothers closer, her heart pounding in her chest. But Hook's voice sliced through the stillness like a blade.

"Now!" he roared, and in an instant, the pirates surged forward, their weapons glinting in the firelight. The attack was sudden and brutal. The Lost Boys, caught completely off guard, scrambled to their feet, panic igniting in their eyes. Shouts of surprise and terror filled the air as Hook's men descended upon them, swinging swords and striking down those who were caught off guard.

"Fight back!" Peter shouted, rallying the Lost Boys as he drew his two knives, but the chaos was overwhelming. The sound of clashing metal and anguished cries echoed through the forest, drowning out their screams of defiance. As the pirates struck hard, the battlefield quickly turned into a nightmare.

"Wendy! John! Michael!" Peter cried, trying to gather his friends amidst the chaos. "We need to get out of here!" But even as he fought valiantly, it became clear that the tide was turning against them. The ground was littered with the fallen, the cries of the Lost Boys mingling with the triumphant shouts of Hook's crew. It was a massacre, and the reality of their predicament began to sink in.

"Peter, we have to go!" Wendy urged, her voice breaking as she pulled at his arm, desperation in her eyes. "They're too many!" In that moment, Peter felt a jolt of nervous energy as he searched frantically for Tinkerbell.

"Where's Tink?" he shouted, panic rising in his chest. She had been flitting around them just moments ago, but now, she was nowhere to be seen. Suddenly, a cruel laugh cut through the chaos, and Peter's heart dropped as he turned to see Captain Hook standing triumphantly, holding Tinkerbell tightly in his grasp. Her tiny body struggled against his fingers, her face contorted in horror.

"Look what I have, Pan!" Hook taunted, his eyes gleaming with sadistic joy. "Your precious little fairy."

"No! Let her go!" Peter shouted, his voice cracking with desperation. "You monster!"

With a swift motion, Hook's blade flashed in the firelight, and before Peter could react, Hook slashed Tinkerbell's throat. Time seemed to freeze as the fairy's eyes widened in shock, a soft gasp escaping her lips before she fell limp in Hook's grip, blood spilling like glittering stars against the dark ground.

"Tinkerbell! No!" Peter screamed, anguish tearing through him. His heart shattered into pieces as he watched his dear friend die, the weight of despair crashing down on him. The sound of the battle faded into the background, and all that mattered was the loss of Tinkerbell.

"We have to go! Now!" Wendy shouted. "She's gone, Peter." They summoned the thirteen remaining Lost Boys, their faces pale as they processed the horror of what had just unfolded.

"We can't fight them," John admitted, his voice trembling. "We have to flee." With tears in his eyes, Peter nodded, lifting his knife defiantly, though he knew the battle was lost.

"To the skies, everyone!" He beckoned them to follow, desperation propelling them upward. As they ascended into the air, the world below faded into a blur of chaos. Peter glanced back, his heart heavy with grief and tears running from his eyes as he saw Hook and his men celebrating their victory, the laughter of the pirates ringing cruelly in his ears. With one final look at the forest that had been their sanctuary, their home, Peter and his friends flew away, the burden of loss trailing behind them like a dark shadow. They soared through the night, leaving behind the horrors of the battle, but the memory of Tinkerbell's sacrifice and the devastation of their defeat would haunt them forever.

****

High above the treetops, a cold wind whipped through the air as Peter Pan led the remnants of his crew through the night sky. The stars twinkled like distant lanterns, but their light felt cold and hollow in the wake of their loss. Tinkerbell's lifeless form haunted Peter's thoughts: he could still see her vibrant glow dimming into darkness. Wendy, tightness forming in her chest, glanced at Peter, concern etching deep lines across her brow.

"Peter, where do we go now?" she asked, her voice barely a whisper amidst the rush of wind. "We can't go back to the hideout. Hook will be waiting for us." Peter clenched his jaw, frustration boiling within him.

"I don't know, Wendy! I thought we could always find a way to escape. I thought..." His voice trailed off, the weight of his failure pressing down on him like a stone.

"Peter, we need to regroup and make a plan," Nibs interjected, trying to keep the despair at bay. "We can't let Hook win. Tinkerbell wouldn't want us to give up."

"But how can we fight back?" *Henry*, one of the surviving Lost Boys, added, his voice trembling. "We lost so many of our brothers. We're not strong enough." The group fell silent, the truth of Henry's words hanging in the air like a thick fog. They had suffered a devastating loss, and the laughter and joy they once knew in Neverland felt like a distant memory. As they flew, Peter spotted a secluded glen nestled among the trees, the moonlight spilling over it like a silver blanket.

"There! We can hide there for now. It's away from Hook and his crew." With a gesture, he led them downward, landing softly on the grass. The glen was peaceful, with flowers blooming in the moonlight and a gentle stream flowing nearby. But the serene beauty did little to soothe the ache in their hearts. Peter turned to the group, his expression determined but hollow.

As they settled down, the weight of their loss hung heavily over them like a dark cloud. Peter felt numb as he looked at the faces of his friends, their eyes filled with both grief and fear. He took a deep breath, trying to steady his voice as he addressed the group.

"We need to regroup and figure out our next move. But first, there's something you all need to know." Wendy knelt beside Peter, her brow furrowed with concern.

"What is it, Peter?" she asked.

"We've run out of fairy dust," Peter said, his voice strained. "Without it, we won't be able to fly for much longer. We'll lose our only advantage against Hook." Gasps rippled through the group as they did not consider that as a possible outcome. The reality of their situation hit them hard; without the ability to fly, they would be vulnerable and trapped. Michael's face paled, and he clutched at his brother's arm.

"What do we do now?" Tootles asked, fear evident in his voice. One of the Lost Boys, an athletic-looking lad named *Nibs*, stepped forward, his eyes brightening with an idea.

"What if we travel to the *Land of the Fairies*?" he suggested.

"Great idea, Nibs," Curly agreed.

"Yeah," replied Swervy, "we could seek out Tinkerbell's mother, the *Fairy Queen*! She might help us regain our fairy dust and give us the strength to fight back against Hook!" The suggestion hung in the air, sparking a flicker of hope among the group. But another Lost Boy, *Slightly,* older and more cautious, shook his head vigorously.

"That's madness! *The Land of the Fairies* is to the west, and it's filled with monsters and undead creatures. Traveling there on foot is a death sentence. We'd be walking straight into danger!"

"Perhaps we should stay hidden until we can find another way," *Tootles* said, glancing nervously at the surrounding trees.

"We can't risk it." Peter's resolve hardened as he listened to the protests. He stepped forward, his eyes blazing with determination. "I understand the risks of going west, but we can't just hide forever. Tinkerbell is gone, and we owe it to her to fight back. If we don't regain our ability to fly, we'll always be on the run, always looking over our shoulders. And one day, Hook and his men will catch us, and they will kill us."

"And he will kill us all slowly," Curly said, agreeing with Peter.

"We can't let Hook win!" Peter shouted. Wendy placed a comforting hand on Peter's shoulder, her heart swelling with admiration for his courage.

"We should go to the *Land of the Fairies.* We should honor Tinkerbell's memory by fighting for her. She would want us to be brave." The Lost Boys exchanged glances, the gravity of the decision weighing heavily on them. John stepped forward, his voice steady.

"If we're going to do this, we need to stick together. We can't afford to lose anyone else." Peter nodded, unyielding resolve gleaming in his eyes.

"We will stay united. We'll face whatever comes our way together... For Tinkerbell!" Knuckles shouted. With their spirits slightly lifted, the group reluctantly agreed to the plan. They gathered their courage and prepared for the journey ahead.

"Alright, let's set out," Peter commanded, his voice strong and unwavering. "We'll head west, and we'll stay alert. Remember, we're doing this for Tinkerbell, for Neverland, and for the ones we lost as well as our very survival!"

As the darkness overtook the dense forest, Peter Pan and his loyal crew glided silently through the air, their playful laughter replaced by an unsettling hush. Each heartbeat echoed in their ears as they approached a small clearing, barely visible through the thick canopy of leaves, where the gentle murmur of the nearby water seemed to whisper secrets of impending trouble.

"Stay close," Peter urged, glancing back at the group. "We can't afford to get separated."

Wendy flew beside him, her heart racing with anxiety.

"Do you really think Tinkerbell's mother will help us?" she asked, her voice barely above a whisper. Peter nodded, his eyes fixed ahead.

"I believe she will. Tinkerbell was important to her, and if we tell her what happened, she'll understand our need for help."

Chapter 4

Skull Creek

The thick darkness of night cloaked Neverland in shadows, the moon casting a silvery glow over the dense foliage. Peter Pan and the group gathered in a small clearing, the atmosphere brimming with apprehension. The chirping of crickets and the rustle of leaves surrounded them as they huddled close.

"We need a plan to reach the *Land of the Fairies*," Peter declared, his voice steady despite the looming uncertainty. "But we have to be careful. The fairy dust is almost gone." Slightly looked around at the faces of the boys, his brow furrowed in thought.

"What if we walk to *Skull Creek* first? It's only about a hundred yards away. That way, we can save our fairy dust for when we actually need to fly."

"Good idea, Slightly!" Curly replied, nodding eagerly. "Then we can fly low and fast across the creek!"

"Yeah, but it's still going to be dangerous," Tootles interjected, adjusting his shirt nervously. "The creek is filled with crocodiles just waiting for a chance to snap us out of the air."

"Tootles, you're right!" Peter said. "We need to stick together and be quick. Once we get to the edge, I'll give the signal to go." The boys exchanged wary glances, but they didn't have many options left.

"Let's do it!" Nubs exclaimed, enthusiasm rising in the group. With renewed ambition, they set off, the darkness wrapping around them like a blanket. They attempted to walk softly, but as children, they couldn't help but create a commotion. Furthermore, they weren't accustomed to walking long distances since they were used to flying. The path was illuminated by the gentle glow of the moon above, guiding them toward the creek. As they approached the edge of *Skull Creek*, the sound of water rushing over stones filled the air, mingling with the distant growls of the crocodiles lurking beneath the surface. The boys halted, peering into the inky blackness of the water, their pulses quickened.

"Alright, everyone," Peter said, his voice firm and confident. "This is it. We need to be brave. Stay close, and remember the plan. We'll fly low and fast."

"Just a few feet above the water," Michael whispered, his eyes wide as he stared at the dark ripples. "Right?"

"Exactly!" Peter replied, his own excitement bubbling just beneath the surface. "On my count, we take off together. *One... two... three!*"

With that, Peter leaped into the air, the group following suit. They soared upward, the rush of wind filling their lungs as they glided just above the water's surface. The moonlight shimmered off the creek, casting an ethereal glow around them.

"Go, go, go!" Peter shouted, pushing them forward as they reached the center of the creek. They were halfway across, and still flying smoothly. The thrill of flying mingled with the fear of the hungry crocodiles below, their eyes shimmering in the darkness. "Faster, everyone!" Peter shouted with excitement and urgency. "We need to make it across before the dust wears off!" Wendy flapped her arms, urging the Lost Boys onward.

"We can do this! Just keep your eyes on the other side!" Wendy shouted.

As they raced forward, the wind whipped through their hair, and the thrill of the chase sent adrenaline coursing through their veins. Below them, the crocs snapped their jaws, the sounds echoing ominously, but most of the gang was too focused on their flight to notice the danger beneath. Tootles, however, looked down in terror as a crocodile jumped out of the water and snapped its jaws just below his feet as he glided by.

Suddenly, with only about fifty yards to shore, a gasp broke the air as Curly faltered, his body fluttering erratically.

"Peter! I can't—" Before he could finish, he dropped like a stone, splashing into the water below.

"Curly!" cried Nibs, his eyes widening in horror. But before anyone could react,

Tootles wobbled, and he too tumbled toward the creek, disappearing beneath the surface. Most didn't notice right away; they were too wrapped up in their own urgency. Suddenly, eight more Lost Boys fell perilously into the water. One fell right into the mouth of a hungry crocodile. His terrifying screams alerted the rest of the group as several crocodiles feasted on him.

Some had made it to shore by now. It was then that they began to realize that not everyone had made it across, and the frantic energy shifted into a chaotic scramble. Some were still in flight on their way to shore. The boys in the water fought to swim toward the shore, struggling against the current and their own fear.

"Swim! Get to the shore!" Curly yelled, his voice filled with desperation. But the hungry crocodiles had been waiting. With a terrifying swiftness, one lunged at one of the boys, its jaws wide open.

"No! Not like this!" he screamed, his voice cut short as he was dragged under, leaving only a whirl of bubbles in his wake.

"Look back!" John shouted, pulling Michael close as they raced for the shore.

"We have to help them!"

Wendy turned, her heart sinking as she saw several Lost Boys thrashing in the water, their cries drowned out by the splashes of the crocodiles circling hungrily.

"Peter! They're in trouble!"

"Go! Get to the shore!" Peter commanded, his breathing intensifying as he turned back toward the water. "I'll save them!"

In an instant, the water erupted as a massive crocodile lunged from the depths, jaws wide open, its jaws snapping open and clamping down on *Jake's* torso, the sickening crunch of bone echoing through the water. He flailed helplessly, screams swallowed by the murky depths as the creature dragged him under, leaving only bubbles and ripples where he once stood. Panicked, *Thomas* and *Leo* turned and swam for their lives, but another crocodile surged forward, jaws wide, and caught Leo by the leg, its powerful grip yanking him beneath the surface, the boy's terrified cries muffled by the rush of water. As Leo vanished, Thomas continued swimming furiously, but a third crocodile emerged from the shadows, clamping its jaws shut around his waist with a vicious snap, pulling him into the dark depths as he fought against the unyielding force. The water churned violently, filled with splashes and desperate struggles. The air swelling with urgency as Peter raced toward the struggling boys, his heart in his throat.

"Hang on! I'm coming!" he shouted, but the crocs were quick, their jaws snapping just inches from the bobbing heads of his friends. Below, Curly and Tootles were struggling, their arms flailing as they tried to swim. The crocs lunged, their powerful jaws snapping close enough to send chills down Peter's spine.

"Help!" Tootles cried, his voice laced with fear.

"Hold on! I'll get you!" Nibs shouted, heart beating furiously as he dove down toward him. Nibs reached for Tootles just as a croc lunged for him, hoisted him up on his back, and flew to shore. Slightly and Knuckles flew back and scooped Henry and Swervy from the water, carrying them on their backs to safety.

As Peter swooped low, he reached

for Curly, who was slipping beneath the water's surface. "Grab my hand!" Peter yelled, stretching out his arm. With a desperate lunge, Curly latched onto Peter's wrist, and with a surge of strength, Peter pulled him up.

The one remaining Lost Boy, *Hands*, scrambled to the safety of the bank. With one final surge of energy, he broke free of the water, scrambling up onto the shore where John and Michael reached out, pulling him to safety. But the water was now a scene of chaos, cries echoing as the crocs feasted on the Lost Boys who had fallen, the tragic cost of their adventure laid bare before them.

"Five of our friends..." Michael whispered, tears brimming in his eyes.

Wendy's heart ached, her voice trembling. "We have to remember them. They were brave."

Peter stood at the water's edge, a sense of dread surrounding him as he glanced back at the rippling surface. "We'll carry their spirits with us. We won't forget."

With that promise hanging in the air, the group turned, united in their grief but resolute to honor their friends as they continued their journey, the *Land of the Fairies* awaiting them beyond the horizon.

****

The moon hung high and full, casting an eerie glow over *Skull Creek*, where shadows clung to the jagged rocks like dark secrets. *Captain Hook* stood at the edge of the creek, the spot where the group had taken flight just moments earlier, his sharp eyes narrowing as he watched the tumultuous scene unfold across the water. Peter Pan and his crew were struggling to navigate the treacherous shallows, their laughter now tinged with panic. Just moments before, the night had turned gruesome, with the sounds of splashing and frantic cries echoing as five Lost Boys fell victim to the lurking crocodiles, their echoes swallowed by the dark waters.

"Look at them, floundering like fools!" Hook sneered, a wicked gleam in his eye. "They think they can escape me, but they're nothing without their flying tricks."

"Captain, they're headed west!"

shouted the rough-looking pirate named Mullins as he peered through the darkness with keen interest. "But what could be over there? There is nothing but death and despair in the west. It could be a trap."

"Or a hideout," another pirate chimed in, his voice low. "They might think they're safe, but they're just leading us to their next blunder."

"Safe?" Hook scoffed, his voice dripping with sarcasm. "They're as good as caught. Look at them now! They can't fly, and their precious Lost Boys are nothing but a snack for the crocs. If they thought they could escape on foot, they've made a grave mistake."

He turned sharply to his crew, his expression fierce. "Signal *The Jolly Roger*! We'll follow them like shadows. They may think they're clever, but they have no idea how much easier they've made it for us. They're trapped!"

As the crew scrambled to light a signal, the flickering flames illuminated their eager faces, reflecting their anticipation. Hook's eyes remained locked on the chaos across the creek, where Peter struggled to regroup his remaining crew, panic etched on his youthful face.

"Captain, what if they know we're watching?" Smee asked, his voice trembling slightly.

"They've lost their ability to fly, Smee!" Hook snapped, a cruel smile forming on his lips. "They're just a pack of frightened children now. They've given up their advantage, and it's only a matter of time before we catch them."

"Fools! They think they can outrun the darkness!" Hook roared, his laughter reverberating through the night. "They'll wish they had never set foot in this cursed place once I'm done with them."

As the signal blazed brightly in the night sky, Hook felt a surge of exhilaration. *The Jolly Roger* would soon be there, and the hunt would intensify.

"Ready yourselves, men! We'll follow them into the depths of their despair," Hook commanded, his voice forceful and fierce. "Soon, we feast on the sweet taste of victory!"

With that, the pirates rallied, the thrill of the chase igniting their spirits. Hook grinned, anticipation crackling in the air as he envisioned the impending chaos and the inevitable capture of Peter Pan and his crew, lost and vulnerable beneath the unforgiving gaze of the moonlit sky.

****

The flickering flames of the campfire cast a warm glow against the night, a small sanctuary in the midst of darkness. Peter Pan, Wendy, John, Michael, and the *eight* remaining Lost Boys huddled together on the banks of Skull Creek, their hearts heavy with the loss of their five friends to the crocodiles lurking in the depths.

Hands, one of the Lost Boys who remained silent, was teaching Michael sign language. Though *Hands* could hear perfectly well and was capable of speaking, he felt shy about using his voice because he wasn't confident in his speaking ability.

"Gather close, everyone," Peter said, his voice steady despite the fear that gripped them. "We need to regroup and plan our next move. We're headed west to *The Land of the Fairies*, but first, we must face *The Tower of Shadows*." Wendy pulled her cloak tighter around her shoulders, glancing at the flickering fire.

"What's so dangerous about this tower, Peter?" Slightly, ever eager to share a tale, leaned in closer to the firelight.

"I've heard whispers about *The Shadow King* who lives there. They say he has eyes everywhere and can trap anyone who dares enter his domain." Tootles shivered, his voice barely above a whisper as he uttered, "And his loyal servants are said to be the shadows of lost souls, forever bound to do his bidding. They creep around the tower, searching for anyone who wanders too close." Nibs nodded vigorously, his eyes wide.

"I heard they can steal your very essence, leaving you as nothing but a shadow yourself! You'd be trapped there forever, like the poor souls who never escaped!" Curly chimed in, his voice trembling with fear.

"And some say that if you listen closely, you can hear the cries of those who were taken... cries that echo in the night!"

"And it is always dark there, even the

nearby areas are in perpetual darkness," Swervy announced.

The group sat in silence for a moment, the crackling of the fire the only sound breaking the heavy atmosphere. Peter, sensing their fear, leaned forward, his expression spirited.

"But we must not give in to fear. *The Shadow King* is an enemy of *Captain Hook*. If we can bargain with him, he might let us pass unharmed."

"Bargain with an evil king?" John questioned, his brow furrowed. "What could we possibly offer him?" Peter thought for a moment, his mind racing.

"We can offer him information about Hook. We can tell the king that we have come to warn him that Hook and his men are on their way to defeat him in an effort to take over the west, and if we present ourselves as allies against Hook, it could be enough to earn our passage."

"But what if he doesn't care?" Knuckles asked, his voice quaking. "What if we end up trapped like the others?"

"Then we'll have to be clever," Peter replied, determination shining in his eyes.

"We're not just any lost boys and girls—we're the ones who can outsmart even the darkest of foes. We can do this together."

The fire crackled, sending sparks flying into the night sky once more, and the group felt a flicker of hope amidst their fear. They exchanged glances, knowing the danger ahead but also the strength they held in their unity.

"We should probably get some rest until morning," Henry suggested.

"Morning?" Nibs responded sarcastically.

"Yeah, daylight," John chimed in.

"There is no sunlight for miles and miles past the Shadow King's domain," Peter mentioned.

"Yeah," Slightly said, "there won't be sunlight until we get closer to The Land of the Fairies, where there is only sunlight, no darkness."

"I meant we just need some rest," Henry corrected himself.

"Rest?" Curly responded. "We can't rest. Hook is probably right on our tails."

Wendy sat up straight, a look of confusion covering her face.

"But wait," she said. "I thought that Tinkerbell's mom was the ruler of the west?" Peter explains to Wendy the backstory between the two opposing forces.

The shadows and fairies exist as two opposing forces within their mystical realm, each embodying the potent elements of light and darkness. The fairies, radiant beings of luminescence, harness the power of light to nurture and sustain their environment. Their glow is not merely decorative; it serves as a weapon against the shadows, which are rendered vulnerable and weak in the presence of fairy light. For the shadows, this light is lethal, capable of dispersing their forms and weakening their hold on the world. Conversely, the shadows thrive in darkness, where their influence grows, creating an atmosphere of fear and despair. This darkness poses a significant threat to the fairies, who risk losing their magic and vitality if they stray too far into shadowy territories. They are virtually invincible in sunlight, but they grow significantly weaker at night. The very nature of these two entities creates an atmosphere of mutual fear and respect, with each keenly aware that any confrontation could lead to devastating consequences for both sides.

To ensure their survival, the fairies and shadows have established a tenuous peace by occupying opposite ends of the western realm. This geographical division serves as a protective barrier, allowing each side to flourish without the constant threat of annihilation from the other. The fairies inhabit vibrant clearings filled with sunlight, where their magic can thrive, while the shadows lurk in dark forests and caverns, where they can exert their influence without interference. Although this arrangement appears peaceful, it is rooted in a profound fear of confrontation. Both factions share legends and warnings about the dangers of crossing into each other's territories, tales that serve to reinforce their boundaries and maintain the fragile balance between light and dark. In this way, their coexistence is a dance of self-preservation, as they navigate their existence with the knowledge that a single misstep could plunge them into conflict, threatening to unravel the delicate order of their world.

"Alright," Wendy said, her voice steady. "We'll face *The Tower of Shadows* together. We'll find a way to outsmart *The Shadow King* and make it to *The Land of the Fairies*."

"Together!" the Lost Boys echoed, their voices rising with belief.

As the fire burned brightly, the group knew they needed to keep moving as Captain Hook and his men couldn't be that far behind. They remained quiet, lacking their typical laughter and playful exchanges, knowing they would need every ounce of strength and courage they could muster for the journey ahead. The shadows whispered around them, but together, they were ready to face whatever horrors lay in store at *The Tower of Shadows*.

Chapter 5

Tower of Shadows

The air was charged with anxiety as Peter Pan, Wendy, John, Michael, and the eight Lost Boys stood at the edge of the heart of the west, their eyes fixed on the ominous silhouette of the *Tower of Shadows*. The structure loomed like a dark giant, its jagged edges clawing at the darkened sky. A large, weathered fence surrounded it, with a gaping hole just wide enough for them to slip through.

In the area surrounding the *Tower of Shadows*, an eternal night blankets the land, casting a somber veil over the jagged landscape. Gnarled trees, their branches twisted like skeletal fingers, reach out from the ground, shrouded in a twirling mist that clings to the earth like a mournful ghost. The air is laden with an oppressive silence, broken only by the occasional rustle of shadows, which flit between the trees like whispers of lost souls. At the heart of this desolate expanse stands the Tower, a monolithic structure of dark stone that seems to absorb the very light around it, its summit lost in the swirling clouds above. The Shadow King, an enigmatic figure cloaked in darkness, rules this bleak territory with an iron grip, his presence felt rather than seen, as he commands a legion of shadows that patrol the land ceaselessly. These dark sentinels glide through the night, their forms ever-shifting, ensuring that no flicker of hope dares to pierce the somber veil that envelops the Tower and its forsaken realm.

"Listen up, everyone," Peter whispered, his voice low but urgent. "We need to be quiet and quick. The shadows are patrolling this area, and if they see us, we'll have to negotiate—something I'd rather avoid." Wendy nodded, squeezing Michael's shoulder reassuringly.

"Stick close together. We can do this," Peter said.

They took deep, ragged breathes as they crawled through the hole in the high fence, one by one, emerging on the other side into a realm of whirling darkness and flickering silhouettes. The ground was uneven, littered with sharp stones that crunched beneath their feet. The shadows danced around them, shifting and twisting like living creatures, their hollow eyes scanning the area.

"Look!" John pointed ahead. A pair of shadows flitted past, their forms elongated and distorted, murmuring secrets to one another in hushed tones. "We need to go around them quietly."

The eerie sounds of the Shadows' whispers and screeches covered the air like a chilling fog, a haunting symphony of low, guttural mumbles interspersed with sharp, piercing shrieks. Their whispers slithered through the darkness, an unintelligible language that seemed to weave in and out of the shadows, echoing with a sinister rhythm that was extremely unnerving. Each screech pierced the stillness, a jagged sound reminiscent of nails scraping against a chalkboard, reverberating with an unsettling echo that felt as though it could slice through the silence of the night.

Together, they created a dissonant lullaby, a chorus of dread that filled the heart with an instinctual fear, warning of the unseen dangers lurking just beyond the veil of darkness.

They ducked behind a cluster of knotted roots, their breaths held tight in their chests. As the shadows approached, they could see the sharp angles of their bodies, the way they seemed to flicker in and out of existence. The boys watched, wide-eyed, as one of the shadows reached out, its fingers stretching like dark tendrils in the air.

"Stay still!" Peter urged, his voice barely above a whisper. They pressed against the rough bark, hearts racing as the shadows passed just inches away, their whispers sending shivers down their spines. Once the coast was clear, they crept further into the grounds, moving in a low crouch. Suddenly, Tootles stumbled, his foot catching on a hidden root. The thud echoed like a drum, and they all froze.

"Shh!" Peter hissed, turning to see the shadows whip around, their attention drawn. "Hide!"

They scrambled behind a thicket, but it was too late. A pair of shadows, larger and more menacing than the others, converged on their position, their forms solidifying into something distinctly threatening.

Wendy's veins pulsed with intensity as she whispered, "Peter, what do we do?" Peter stepped forward bravely, raising his chin.

"We don't mean any harm. We're here to see *The Shadow King*."

Before they could react, the shadows lunged forward, capturing them in a sweeping darkness. The air was heavy and cold as they were surrounded, their cries muffled by the weight of the shadows pressing in.

"Peter!" Michael shouted, panic rising in his voice.

"Stay calm!" Peter shouted back, determination igniting in his eyes. "Remember our plan. Let me do the talking."

The shadows held them tightly, their forms swirling around the children and dragging them like prisoners into the tower.

As they were pulled deeper into the heart of the Tower, their bodies trembled with the terror that awaited them.

****

At the heart of the Tower lies the *Shadow Throne*, a seat carved from the very essence of darkness, where the King presides over his court of shadows. Here, he weaves dark magic and plots against the flickering light of distant lands, for he yearns to expand his dominion beyond the boundaries of his realm. The shadows, ever-watchful and ever-loyal, wait for his command, ready to plunge the world deeper into despair should he desire it.

Peter Pan stood at the forefront, flanked by Wendy, John, Michael, and the remaining Lost Boys—Nibs, Tootles, Curly, Slightly, Knuckles, Swervy, Henry, and Hands. They were trapped and terrified as they came face to face with *The Shadow King*, a looming figure of darkness with no discernible features and an endless void where his eyes should be. *The Shadow King* growled, his voice resonating like distant thunder, reverberating through the chamber.

"What do we have here? Intruders in the domain of the Tower?" With a deep breath, Peter stepped forward, mustering every ounce of courage.

"Your Majesty," he began, his voice steady yet laced with urgency. "We traveled from far away, losing many boys along the way, just to warn you that *Captain Hook* is plotting to take over the west. He is headed this way, seeking to defeat you in battle!" The Shadow King paused, the shadows around him swirling in contemplation. Peter's crew trembled in silence, eyes wide with fear, but Peter remained resolute, his gaze fixed on the dark figure before him.

"Captain Hook?" the Shadow King echoed, his voice low and menacing, as if the very walls of the tower quaked in response. "That fool could never hope to defeat me! Why have you come all this way to say this? What does it matter to you?"

Peter hesitated, caught off guard by the king's question.

"With all due respect, Your Majesty, we face a shared adversary. Captain Hook has been scheming for my downfall for many years, as you may know." The king grunted in acknowledgment. "If he were to triumph over you, it would make it much simpler for him to reach me. You could even say we're allies," Peter admitted reluctantly. The Shadow King was taken aback by Peter's frankness.

"Allies?" he growled, a mix of anger and amusement in his voice. "We are not allies, BOY! What's to prevent me from ending your life right now and enslaving your shadows for eternity, which would please me greatly?" The group quivered in fear.

"I had hoped you would appreciate my gesture in coming all this way to offer my assistance, Your Grace."

"Hmm," the king mused, pausing for a moment.

"And where is your little fairy?" the king asked sarcastically. "The one who always travels with you?" Peter's heart raced, but he kept his composure.

"Tinkerbell?" he replied. "I wouldn't dream of bringing her here, Your Highness," he said, bowing his head slightly in a show of false respect. "She's far too fragile for such a dark place, and I wouldn't want to offend you." The Shadow King's presence seemed to shift, the shadows around him pausing in their restless dance.

"You show respect, boy. I will take that into consideration." He leaned closer, the darkness around him churning with curiosity. "And because of your information, I will allow you to pass through my domain safely." Peter felt a flicker of hope as the tension in the room began to ease. The others breathed a sigh of relief.

"Thank you, Your Excellence," he said, then turned back to his friends and gave them a subtle wink to assure them of their escape. As they began to move toward the exit, a shadow detached itself from the larger mass and slinked across the floor, whispering in a dark, hissing tone.

"My King, they come! Captain Hook and his men approach!" The atmosphere shifted again, a charge of emotions filling the air as the Shadow King's form seemed to swell with ominous energy.

"So, they dare to tread upon my territory?" he growled, his voice a storm of fury. Peter's heart raced again, but he kept his composure, sensing that their moment of deception was nearing its end.

"We must hurry!" he urged, glancing back at his friends, their expressions fearful but determined.

"Flee, then," the Shadow King commanded, his voice echoing off the walls as shadows began to converge, creating a swirling vortex around him. "But know this: if Hook dares to invade my realm, he will face a darkness he cannot comprehend!"

With that, Peter and the others sprinted away, their bodies buzzed not just from fear, but from the thrill of their narrow escape. As they dashed through the winding corridors of the Tower of Shadows, the threat of Captain Hook loomed ever closer, but for now, they had outsmarted the darkness, at least for the moment.

****

As Captain Hook and his ragtag army of pirates approached the foreboding Tower of Shadows, a cold mist seeped through the air, curling around their ankles like ghostly tendrils. The dark edifice loomed above them, its jagged silhouette cutting into the night sky. Hook, with his signature hat tilted jauntily and a gleam of ambition in his eye, strode confidently toward the towering gates, his men trailing behind, feeling both trepidation and skepticism.

"Are you sure about this, Captain?" one of the pirates, a burly man with a scruffy beard, asked, his voice quivering slightly. "Just waltzing up to the Shadow King like we own the place? What if he doesn't take kindly to our intrusion?" Hook waved a dismissive hand, his confidence unshaken.

"Nonsense! We are here with a purpose. What could possibly go wrong? We'll simply explain that we're on the hunt for that wretched Peter Pan. Surely, even the Shadow King would want to rid his domain of such a pest."

The crew grumbled, exchanging nervous glances, but Hook pressed forward, with a hook on one hand and his sword at his side. As they crossed the threshold into the shadowy grounds, the shadows began to twitch and writhe, as if alive and aware of the intruders. Suddenly, dark figures sprang from the ground, swirling like smoke come to life. The shadows surged toward the pirates, a chaotic mass of blackness that sliced through the air like knives. One pirate screamed as a shadowy tendril wrapped around his throat, dragging him down into the dark abyss. His body convulsed momentarily before falling limp, his face frozen in terror.

"Back! Back!" shouted another crew member, raising his cutlass in a futile defense. But more shadows swarmed, slashing at him with razor-like precision. He staggered backward, his cries cut short as a dark form engulfed him, leaving only a whisper of despair in its wake.

"Fight them off! Fight!" Hook bellowed, his bravado weakening as he witnessed the carnage unfolding around him. Shadows twisted and coiled, lunging at the remaining pirates with a ferocity that was both mesmerizing and horrifying. One pirate, desperate to escape, ran for the gates, but a shadow erupted from the ground, ensnaring his legs and dragging him down, his screams echoing off the stone walls.

"Captain, we can't hold them!" another pirate yelled, his face pale with fear. He swung his sword wildly, cleaving through the darkness, but only a few shadows dissipated, seeming to laugh at his futile attempts.

"Retreat! We must retreat!" Hook commanded, his voice now filled with urgency as he fought off a shadow that lashed out at him, narrowly missing his face. He could feel the chill of death creeping closer, and with a swift motion, he turned, leading the frantic flight back toward the entrance. The shadows, relentless and hungry, pursued them with an insatiable thirst for chaos. One last pirate, caught in the fray, was lifted off his feet and suspended in the air as shadows wrapped around him like a funeral shroud.

"Captain! Help me!" he cried, but his plea was swallowed by the darkness as he vanished without a trace. As Hook and the remaining pirates scrambled back through the gates, the shadows coiled back into the earth, leaving behind the echoes of despair and the chilling realization of their defeat. Hook stumbled out, panic overtaking him, the bravado he once wore now replaced by the stark terror of what lay within the *Tower of Shadows.*

"Get to the ship! We've underestimated this place," he panted, urgency lacing his words. "We will sail up the west coast and find another entry point." Hook's men, shaken and terrified, followed his command, knowing that the shadows were not just figments of darkness but a lethal force that would not easily be defeated.

Chapter 6

The Cursed Carnival

The *Cursed Carnival* in Neverland is a desolate echo of its former glory, where remnants of laughter and joy now lie in ruins. Once a vibrant spectacle, the carnival is now a grotesque monument of despair, its bright colors faded to muted tones under the weight of perpetual darkness. The rides, once thrilling and alive with excitement, have succumbed to rust and neglect; the Ferris wheel stands eerily still, its creaking spokes whispering tales of joy that have long turned to sorrow. Games of chance, once bustling with hopeful participants, now sit untouched, their prizes gathering dust, offering only the hollow promise of what once was. Shadows cling to every corner, and the air is thick with the scent of decay, mingling with the chilling remnants of laughter that twist into mournful echoes.

As night perpetually envelops the carnival, the atmosphere grows heavy with an unsettling energy, accentuated by the looming presence of the Tower of Shadows. Its dark spire pierces the sky, casting an unyielding gloom over the carnival grounds, where flickering lights once illuminated the faces of joyous revelers. Frayed tents flap like restless spirits, their colors drained, and the carousel, adorned with chipped and faded horses, stands eerily silent, frozen in a state of hopelessness. The air hums with an otherworldly tension, as if the very ground is steeped in forgotten dreams and lost hopes. In this cursed realm, the laughter of children has twisted into a haunting symphony of grief, creating a poignant reminder of the joy that once thrived but has now been swallowed by the shadows. If headed west, one must venture through this terrifying landmark in order to continue further west.

The night sky was a deep indigo, sprinkled with stars that twinkled like lost dreams above the abandoned carnival. Peter Pan led Wendy, John, Michael, and the eight remaining Lost Boys through the desolate grounds, their voices echoing off the dilapidated structures.

"Stay sharp, everyone," Peter urged, his voice low as they navigated the cracked pavement. "This place feels wrong." Silence prevailed throughout the area, interrupted only by the creaking of rusted metal and steel from the decaying rides.

"Look at that!" Wendy exclaimed, pointing to a rusted Ferris wheel looming in the distance, its once-bright colors faded to ghostly hues. As they ventured deeper, the boys' eyes darted around, searching for any sign of life. Unbeknownst to them, they were being watched.

As they approached the old games area, a flicker of movement caught Henry's eye. A figure emerged from the shadows—a clown, dressed in tattered garb with a painted smile that seemed to shimmer in the dim light. The clown waved a hand, beckoning Henry closer with an exaggerated flourish. "Come play a game!" the silent invitation seemed to say, his eyes twinkling with a mischievous lure.

"Hey, Henry! Don't wander off!" John warned, but Henry was already stepping away from the group, drawn in by the allure of the clown's unspoken promise of fun. The others were too engrossed in their own chatter to notice his absence, their voices drowning out the fading sound of his footsteps.

The clown gestured toward a faded ring toss game, and Henry felt a thrill of excitement wash over him. He was just a few steps away when the atmosphere shifted; the air grew heavy and cold. The clown's smile widened, revealing predatory teeth that glimmered in the shadows. In an instant, the playful spirit vanished, replaced by a chilling intent. Henry froze, realization dawning too late.

"Wait!" he shouted, but the clown lunged forward, and the world around him twisted into chaos. A scream tore from Henry's throat, echoing through the carnival, but it was quickly swallowed by the darkness.

Meanwhile, Peter and the others continued their exploration, unaware of Henry's fate. They stumbled upon a decrepit haunted house, their laughter ringing out as they dared each other to enter. Suddenly, a piercing scream shattered the night, sending a shiver down their spines.

"What was that?" Wendy whispered, her eyes wide with fear.

"Sounded like Henry!" Peter replied, his bravado faltering. "We need to find him!"

They raced toward the sound, but before they could reach the source, a clown emerged from the shadows, a grotesque figure that sent terror coursing through them. He held something aloft, and as they drew closer, horror washed over their faces. It was Henry's severed head, eyes wide in eternal fright, his painted smile forever lost.

"No!" John cried, as the reality of their friend's fate sank in. The clown let out a silent laugh, a haunting melody that echoed through the abandoned carnival.

"Run!" Peter shouted, a surge of adrenaline propelling them forward as clowns began to swarm from the shadows, their maniacal laughter filling the air. The boys unsheathed their knives, gripping them tightly as they fought off two menacing clowns that had leaped out in front of them.

Peter Pan led the way, blood racing through his veins, as Wendy, John, Michael, and the remaining Lost Boys sprinted through the maze of forgotten attractions. Clowns, with their twisted grins and manic laughter, pursued them relentlessly, their painted faces a grotesque mockery of joy.

"We need to find an exit!" Curly cried out.

"Keep running!" Peter shouted, glancing back as he brandished his dagger, its blade glinting in the pale light. The clowns were gaining on them, their wild eyes gleaming with a predatory hunger. The group darted past the dilapidated carousel, its skeletal frame looming like a ghost in the night.

"Over there!" Wendy pointed to a nearby funhouse, its warped mirrors reflecting distorted images of themselves. "We can hide inside!" Without hesitation, they veered toward the entrance, but just as they reached the threshold, a chilling scream pierced the air. Swervy had stumbled, falling behind as the clowns closed in. Panic surged through the group.

"Swervy!" Nibs shouted, his voice filled with terror as he turned to see his friend surrounded. The clowns circled him, their laughter echoing like the tolling of a death knell. Their eyes sparkled with madness, and sharp canine teeth glinted in the moonlight.

"Get away from me!" Swervy cried, brandishing his knife, but the clowns charged forward with a frenzied energy, their movements erratic and unpredictable. He fought desperately, slashing at the air, but their numbers were overwhelming.

"Help! Get them off me!" Swervy cried, his voice strained as the clowns converged around him, their jagged teeth tearing into his flesh as he disappeared beneath them.

"Help him!" cried Knuckles, his voice trembling as he stepped forward, but Peter grabbed his arm, shaking his head.

"We can't! We'll be next!" The sound of gnashing teeth filled the air as the clowns converged on Swervy, their laughter growing louder, warping into a cacophony of chaos.

"No!" John shouted, horror etched

across his face. The sight of Swervy fighting valiantly turned into a nightmare as the clowns clawed at him, their laughter blending with his desperate cries.

"We have to move!" Slightly urged, tugging at Peter's sleeve, but the shock held them in place. They could only watch as the clowns feasted, their grotesque forms illuminated by the moonlight, contorting in a horrifying dance of death amidst the shadows of the carnival.

"Run!" Peter finally shouted, breaking the spell of shock that had gripped them. The echoes of his struggle faded into the night, swallowed by the darkness as the group stood frozen, breathing raggedly. With heavy hearts, they turned away, the screams of their friend and the manic laughter of the clowns ringing in their ears as they plunged deeper into the maze of the carnival, desperate to escape the horrors that lurked in the night.

"There!" Slightly shouted, pointing to a rusted exit sign. "We have to get out of here!" he shouted desperately.

"Go!" Peter urged as he paused and waited for the clowns, his gaze intense.

"Peter, please!" Wendy cried, desperation in her voice. "We can't leave you!"

"I'll catch up! Just go, now!" he insisted, eyes locked on the approaching clowns. The group carried on, reluctantly leaving Peter behind.

As Peter killed another clown with his knife, the sound of the evil clowns' laughter echoed ominously behind him, urging him to think fast. Spotting a large pile of carnival debris—broken wooden planks, rusty metal scraps, and discarded props—he skidded to a halt and quickly strategized. With a surge of adrenaline, he gripped the edge of a heavy, splintered ride sign and heaved it toward the clowns, the sign crashing down with a resounding thud. Then, using every ounce of strength, he pushed against a pile of debris, sending it tumbling into the path of the approaching clowns. The debris scattered and piled up haphazardly, creating a makeshift barrier of chaos that blocked their advance. As the clowns futilely tried to scale the structure, their grotesque faces contorted in frustration, Peter took a moment to glance back at the blockade, ensuring it held, before dashing toward the safety of the exit, his adrenaline racing with the thrill of escape.

Chapter 7

The Jolly Roger cut through the dark waters, the moon casting a silvery glow over the sea as waves lapped gently against the hull. Below deck, the atmosphere was fraught with intensity. Captain Hook sat at his ornate table, fingers steepled beneath his chin, his eyes narrowed in thought. Smee nervously fidgeted with a tattered map, while Mullins leaned against the wall, arms crossed, deep in contemplation.

"Where is that insufferable Pan headed?" Hook growled, breaking the silence. "And why, for the love of all that's wicked, is he unable to fly?"

"Maybe he's lost his touch, Captain," Smee suggested hesitantly, glancing at Hook's scowl.

"Bah! That's not the answer I seek, Smee!" Hook snapped, slamming his fist on the table. The sound echoed through the cramped quarters, making Smee jump. "We must discover his plans."

Just then, a series of loud bangs erupted from the trunk in the corner of the chamber. The sound was frantic, desperate. Hook's head snapped around, his eyes glinting with sudden interest.

"By the stars, what's that racket?" he exclaimed. "Open it!"

Mullins moved swiftly, unfastening the lock and flinging the trunk open. Inside, the battered and bruised lost boy, Harry, struggled against his bindings, his eyes wide with fear and determination.

"Mmph, mmph," cried Harry, his muffled grunts and whimpers caused by the gag over his mouth. Mullins removed the gag momentarily and Harry immediately spoke.

"Please, I cannot be in here any longer!" he shouted, his voice hoarse. "I will help you!"

Hook leaned closer, intrigued. "Speak, boy! What do you know?"

The boy gasped for breath, his heart racing as he met Hook's fierce gaze.

"I heard you say that you killed Tinkerbell. And I heard you say that Peter could not fly."

"Very perceptive," Hook scowled sarcastically. "What of it?"

"Peter and the others... they need *fairy dust* to fly!"

His words hung in the air, a revelation that struck Hook like a bolt of lightning. He exchanged a quick glance with Smee and Mullins, realization dawning.

"Fairy dust..." Mullins murmured, tapping his chin thoughtfully. "If they're looking for that, then they must be headed to *The Land of the Fairies*!" Hook straightened, excitement coursing through him.

"Ah, yes!" Hook exclaimed. "We must get to them before they reach Fairy Land!" he declared, urgency lacing his voice. "Increase the ship's speed! We cannot let Pan escape us again."

"Aye, Captain!" Smee stammered, as he rushed up the stairs, overflowing with emotion.

But as Hook's attention turned back to the lost boy, a cruel smile spread across his face.

"And as for you..." he began, a glint of

malice in his eyes. "We have no further use for your babbling."

"Please, don't do this!" the boy pleaded, desperation seeping into his voice. "I can help you! I can—" Mullins stuffed the gag back in Harry's mouth.

"Enough!" Hook shouted, his voice cold as ice; his patience wearing thin. "Mullins, throw him overboard." Mullins stepped forward, his expression hardening.

"Aye, Captain." He closed the trunk, forgetting to lock it, and carried it abovedeck. Harry's muffled grunts and whimpers escalated in a surge of panic.

Ignoring his unintelligible pleas, Mullins moved to the edge of the ship, Hook's commanding presence urging him on. With a swift, merciless heave, he tossed the trunk into the dark, churning sea.

"Now, let's set sail for The Land of the Fairies!" Hook shouted, his laughter blending with the wind as the Jolly Roger surged forward, a predator in the night, chasing the vanishing hopes of a boy who dared to dream.

****

The moon hung low in the night sky as the boys headed deeper into the dense woods of Neverland. Peter Pan led the way, his heart heavy with the with the loss of so many, while Wendy, John, Michael, and the six remaining Lost Boys—Nibs, Tootles, Curly, Slightly, Knuckles and Hands—followed closely behind. They strode purposefully, each step echoing their commitment to reach the *Land of the Fairies* and deliver the devastating news of Tinkerbell's murder at the hands of Captain Hook.

"It's not much further now," Peter said, his voice steady despite the stress of grief that pressed upon him. "We need to let the fairies know what's happened." Wendy glanced up at him, concern etched on her face.

"Do you think they'll believe us?"

"They will have to," Peter replied, his jaw set. "Tink deserves justice, and they know I would never harm her."

As they moved deeper into the woods, the sound of rustling leaves nearby sent a chill down their spines. Everyone froze, eyes wide with fear.

"What was that?" Michael whispered, clutching Wendy's hand tightly.

"Probably just a rabbit," John said, though his voice quivered with uncertainty.

"Or Hook," Tootles added as he too was on edge, eyes darting around the shadows.

"Let's keep going," Knuckles suggested.

But as they ventured further, the rustling grew louder, transforming into a cacophony of snapping branches and shuffling footsteps. Suddenly, from the shadows, a horde of grotesque, zombie-like creatures burst forth, their eyes glowing with a feral hunger.

"Run!" Peter shouted, a surge of panic igniting his voice.

The group erupted into a frantic sprint, hearts pounding as they dashed through the underbrush. Branches whipped against their skin, and the moonlight flickered through the trees like a warning. The fast-moving creatures snarled behind them, their guttural sounds mingling with the pounding of their own hearts.

"Keep up, everyone!" Peter yelled,

glancing back to ensure they were all together. But in the chaos, Hands, who was trailing behind, stumbled over an exposed root.

"Hands! Come on!" Nibs yelled, glancing back to see Hands trailing far behind, panic etched across his face. But it was too late. The creatures lunged at him.

"Hands!" Nibs shouted, as they descended upon him, teeth gnashing, and Hands' terrified eyes locked onto the group for a fleeting moment before he was engulfed in darkness.

"Don't look back! Just run!" Peter urged, forcing himself to focus on the path ahead. They sprinted deeper into the woods, and spotted a small door nestled between the twisted roots of an ancient tree, half-hidden by twisting vines.

"There!" Curly pointed, desperation fueling his voice. "In there!"

With no time to hesitate, they rushed toward the door, Slightly throwing it open. The small room was dark, filled with the scent of damp earth and moss. One by one, they tumbled inside, breathless and terrified.

"Close it! Quick!" Wendy urged, her eyes wide with fright.

Peter slammed the door shut, his hands shaking as he fumbled to bolt it just in time. The creatures crashed against the door, their grunts and snarls reverberating through the small space, sending shivers down their spines.

"What do we do now?" Slightly gasped, his voice trembling as he pressed against the door, trying to brace it with all his weight.

"We can't stay here forever!" Curly cried, glancing around the room, searching for an escape.

"We are so dead," Knuckles cried.

"We have to think of something," Peter said, his voice steadying even as the door rattled violently. "And fast."

"We can't go back out there," Tootles shouted. "There's too many of them!"

"The door is starting to give way," Slightly shouted as he backed away from it.

Wendy clutched Michael close, her eyes filled with tears. "They are gonna break the door down any minute now!" she yelled, fear wrapping around her like a vice.

"We'll think of something," John said, trying to sound brave, though his voice shook. "We always do." As they stood there terrified, the creatures continued to bang on the door, their grunts growing more frantic. The door began cracking.

Wendy's eyes darted around the room, and she spotted an old lantern hanging from the ceiling.

"Look, up there!" she roared.

"A lantern!" Peter replied, moving with urgency. He climbed onto a small crate and reached for the lantern. As he fumbled with the flint, the door shuddered under the relentless assault, a large crack stretching across its surface like a jagged lightning bolt. The wood splintered menacingly, dark splinters jutting out from the widening fissure, threatening to split the door apart completely.

"Hurry, Peter!" Michael urged, fear etched on his young face.

"Guys, over here!" Nibs shouted as he moved debris out of the way and revealed a trapdoor on the ground with a round steel handle sticking out. "It's a hatch leading us to safety, hopefully." Curiosity sparked, everyone hurried over for a closer view. Meanwhile, Peter had already ignited the lantern. Nibs crouched down and lifted the hatch. Peter directed the light into the opening to explore what lay beyond.

"Stairs," Nibs announced with excitement.

"Where do you think they lead?" Wendy asks.

"Down," Tootles shouts as he moves people out of the way and heads down hastily.

"We must hurry," Peter says as he holds the door open. One by one, they began to descend into the darkness below. Peter, being the last, hesitated at the top. Just as he was about to close the hatch, the door splintered, and the creatures burst through, their ghastly forms silhouetted against the dim light. With his anxiety spiking wildly, Peter hurried down the stairs, slamming the hatch shut just in time to block the terrifying sight behind him.

Chapter 8

The Underground Caverns

The Underground Caverns of Neverland are a vast and eerie maze hidden beneath the surface, a place where shadows dance and whispers echo through the dark. As you enter, the air grows cooler, filled with a dampness that clings to your skin. The caverns are illuminated by bioluminescent fungi that cast an otherworldly glow, revealing walls draped in age-old stalactites and stalagmites, their surfaces glistening with moisture. The labyrinthine tunnels twist and turn, leading deeper into the earth. Some paths are narrow and claustrophobic, while others open into expansive chambers where the echoes of dripping water create a haunting symphony.

"I guess we don't need this anymore," Peter says as he looks at the lantern in his hand. He sets it down and marvels at the wonders of the cave.

"We must be getting close to the Land of the Fairies," Nibs says. "This place is much too nice to be in shadow territory."

"Yeah," just keep your eyes peeled, lads," Peter mentions cautiously.

"Wow, it's beautiful!" Michael whispered, wide-eyed, as he gazed around, mesmerized by the shimmering fungi.

"Beautiful? It's creepy!" Tootles squeaked, his voice trembling slightly. He peered into the darkness, paranoia creeping into his thoughts. "What if there are monsters lurking in the shadows?"

"Monsters?" Nibs scoffed, rolling his eyes. "You're just scared of your own shadow, Tootles. This place is just a cave!"

As they ventured deeper, the soft squelch of their footsteps echoed off the stone walls, but the atmosphere shifted as they stumbled upon a chilling sight: a pile of bones lay crumpled in one corner of the cavern, half-buried in the damp earth. The bones were unmistakably human, pale and glistening in the eerie light.

"W-What is that?" Tootles gasped, his face paling as he took a step back.

"Looks like someone didn't make it out of here," Curly muttered, his brow furrowing in concern.

"Great, just great! Now we're in a bone yard!" Tootles exclaimed, his voice rising in panic. "I told you we shouldn't have come down here!"

Nibs clenched his fists, anger igniting in his eyes. He unsheathed his small knife, the blade catching the dim light. "We can't just stand here! We need to decide where to go. There are several passages, and we can't waste time arguing!"

"Hold on!" John interjected, stepping closer to the pile of bones, inspecting it cautiously. "We need to be smart about this. If there's a monster down here, we don't want to draw attention to ourselves."

"Or get lost in this maze!" Slightly added, glancing nervously at the myriad of tunnels that branched off in every direction. "What if we take a wrong turn? We might end up as part of that pile!"

"Maybe we should split up," suggested Knuckles, his voice steady. "One group can take the left tunnel, and the other can go right. We'll cover more ground."

"Split up? Are you mad?" Wendy replied, her eyes widening. "That's how horror stories start! We should stick together!"

"Yeah, what if something gets one of us?" Michael chimed in, his voice trembling with unease.

"Then we'll fight back!" Nibs shot back, gripping his knife tighter. "We're not just going to stand around and let fear control us!"

"Alright, alright!" Peter said, trying to mediate. "How about we choose one path together? Let's make a decision as a group. We'll take the middle passage. It looks wider and less... bone-y." Tootles shivered, glancing over his shoulder at the pile of bones.

"Middle passage it is, then. But I swear if I see any more bones, I'm out of here!"

With a silent agreement, they moved forward, approaching the middle tunnel, the shadows stretching ominously behind them. The caverns were alive with secrets, and as they stepped into the unknown, a sense of foreboding hung over them, reminding them that adventure often came with a price.

The passage felt endless, the shadows shifting with each step. It was as if the very walls were closing in, amplifying the load of their losses.

"We've lost so many already," Wendy said, her voice barely above a whisper. "I can't stop thinking about Hands and the others."

"Yeah, that's not something I like to remember," Knuckles replied, his tone grim. "That zombie attack was brutal. I still can't believe Hands is gone."

"To think that Tink was right there, and we couldn't save her," Tootles added, his voice cracking. "I can hear her laughter still, like a sweet melody. She was so brave..."

"Brave or not, she's gone now," Nibs snapped, frustration bubbling to the surface. "And now we need to convince the fairies it wasn't our fault."

Curly shook his head. "What do you think the fairies will say when they find out Tink is dead? Especially her mother, the

Fairy Queen. She's going to be furious!"

"Furious? She'll be heartbroken, you dolt!" Slightly retorted. "Tinkerbell was her daughter! They'll blame us for her demise."

"Rightly so," John added, folding his arms. "We were supposed to protect her. We can't face the *Fairy Queen* empty-handed. We need her help, especially if we're going to get more fairy dust."

"Fairy dust!" Michael exclaimed, his eyes lighting up. "Do you think she'll give us a large amount? We need it to fly again, to escape Hook!"

"Not just fly, but to take the fight to him!" Nibs interjected, determination sparking in his voice. "If we can get a big enough supply of fairy dust, we can rally the fairies and take back Neverland!"

"But if she doesn't give us any fairy dust," Slightly said with a grim expression, "we'll have to make the journey back on foot to get home."

"Back through the zombies, clowns, and crocs?" Knuckles responded. "Oh, hell no!"

"Yeah, I'm not going back there on foot," Tootles mentioned apprehensively.

"That Shadow King will never let us through again."

Wendy frowned, her expression pensive. "But how do we convince the *Fairy Queen*? She's not just going to hand it over after losing her daughter."

"We'll have to show her we're sorry," Curly suggested. "Maybe if we promise to avenge Tink, she'll see we're serious."

"Yeah, but how can we prove ourselves?" Tootles asked, fear creeping back into his voice. "We can barely even navigate these tunnels, let alone face Hook again."

"Listen," Peter said, his voice growing more resolute. "We've faced danger before, and we can do it again. We will make it through this! We're the Lost Boys, remember? We fight for our own, and we never give up!"

As Peter Pan and the group continued through the middle tunnel, the path opened into a vast chamber filled with a dizzying array of passageways. The walls, still glimmering with bioluminescent fungi, seemed to pulsate with an unsettling energy, illuminating the confusion on their faces.

"Which way do we go?" Tootles asked, his voice quivering with anxiety. "There are too many choices!"

"I don't know! This is ridiculous!" Nibs exclaimed, running a hand through his hair in frustration. "We just need to get the hell out of here already!"

Suddenly, a chilling hiss slithered through the air, followed by a series of ominous whooshing sounds that echoed like distant thunder. The group froze, their gazes filled with trepidation. Huddled together, they strained to listen, the sound growing louder and more menacing.

"What is that?" Curly whispered, his voice barely above a breath. Before anyone could respond, the *Gloom Wyrm* emerged from the shadows, a massive serpent-like creature whose scales absorbed the light around it, leaving only its glowing green eyes visible.

The *Gloom Wyrm* is not just a beast of brute strength; it's cunning and stealthy, often using the winding tunnels to ambush those who wander too far from safety. It paused, studying the group with a menacing stare that sent shivers down their spines.

"Don't move!" Peter commanded, trying to maintain a semblance of calm. "Stay still and don't panic."

But Tootles, overwhelmed by fear, couldn't hold his ground. "I can't! I can't do this!" he shouted, turning on his heel and bolting down the left tunnel.

"Wait! Tootles!" Peter yelled, but it was too late. The rest, gripped by a primal instinct to flee, followed suit, sprinting after Tootles into the dark passage.

The tunnel was narrow, the soft glow of the fungi flickering as they ran, their hearts pounding in sync with their hurried footsteps. Water, ankle-deep and cold, splashed around them, reflecting the ghostly light and creating a slippery surface beneath their feet. The sound of their frantic breaths filled the air, mingling with the distant hissing of the Gloom Wyrm closing in behind them.

"Keep going!" John shouted, trying to maintain their momentum. "We have to outrun it!"

As they navigated the winding tunnels, the water splashed violently with each step, making it hard to maintain their footing. The sound of the Wyrm's hisses grew louder, echoing off the walls and filling the cavern with an acute sense of dread.

"Turn left!" Nibs yelled as they approached a fork in the tunnel. "That way!"

They veered left, the path narrowing even further, the air growing denser with the creature's relentless pursuit. But the terror was not without its cost; Knuckles stumbled, his foot catching on a slick stone, sending him sprawling into the water.

"Knuckles!" Curly shouted, reaching back, but it was too late. The Gloom Wyrm lunged forward, its massive jaws opening wide, revealing rows of razor-sharp teeth. In an instant, it caught Knuckles in its clutches, and a horrifying scream echoed through the tunnel as the creature violently struck, chomping down on Knuckles before spitting him out and continuing the chase.

"No! Knuckles!" Tootles cried, his voice breaking as he pushed forward with the others, desperation driving them onward.

With adrenaline coursing through their veins, they raced toward a large, illuminated hole up ahead, the bright light contrasting sharply against the darkness of the tunnels.

"Look! It's sunlight!" Peter shouted, hope igniting within him. "We have to jump!"

Without hesitation, they approached the edge of a steep cliff that dropped off into the unknown, the wyrm hot on their tails. The cold water below shimmered invitingly, a stark contrast to the terror that chased them. With no time to think, they leaped off the 50-foot drop, plunging into the frigid depths below. The Gloom Wyrm stopped at the edge and watched them fall, seeming almost indifferent about not catching them.

The shock of the cold water hit them, and they flailed momentarily before surfacing, gasping for air. The sunlight above blinded them after being in the dark for so long. But still, the bright light that illuminated the surface was a welcomed sight, although the horrors of the cavern were still fresh in their minds.

"Did we lose it?" John asked, panting as he treaded water, eyes darting back toward the cliff.

"I don't know! We have to swim!" Peter urged, his voice cutting through the panic. "We need to get away from here!"

As they paddled frantically away from the cliff, the sound of the *Gloom Wyrm's* hissing faded, but the loss of Knuckles weighed heavily on their hearts. They had escaped danger, but at what cost?

Chapter 9

The Final Leg

As the Lost Boys settled onto the soft grass at the edge of the shallow creek, the gentle sound of water lapping against the stones provided a soothing backdrop to their weariness. They dried off in the warm sunlight, the golden rays kissing their damp skin as they caught their breath. The landscape around them was enchanting, a vivid display of Neverland's magic.

The creek sparkled under the bright sun, its clear water reflecting the brilliant hues of the wildflowers that danced at its banks. Vibrant blues, purples, and yellows dotted the lush greenery, while the air was filled with the sweet scent of blooming petals. Towering trees with thick trunks and sprawling branches framed the scene, their leaves rustling softly in the breeze. In the distance, the majestic outline of the mountainous rock loomed, its steep face casting a long shadow over the valley.

"We're so close to the *Land of the Fairies*," Wendy said, her gaze filled with wonder as she took in the beauty surrounding them. "It's breathtaking here."

"Yeah, but that climb looks pretty dangerous," Nibs replied, squinting toward the rocky incline. "What if we slip?"

Curly nodded, his brow furrowed with concern. "It's not just steep; it looks unstable too. We could fall if we're not careful."

"Maybe we can find another way around?" Slightly suggested, his voice laced with uncertainty. He glanced at the mountain, then back at the group. "There might be an easier path we haven't seen yet."

Wendy sighed, the plight of their situation settling heavily on her shoulders. "But what if there isn't? We need to get to the Fairy Queen and ask for her help."

Peter, who had been listening quietly, stood up, brushing grass off his clothes. "I'm going to take a walk," he announced, a hint of purpose in his voice. "I need to see if there's a better vantage point to scope out the mountain." Sensing his need for companionship, Wendy immediately rose to follow him.

"I'll come with you," she said, eager to support him in any way she could.

****

As they walked along the creek, the sunlight filtered through the leaves above, casting playful shadows on the ground. The sound of rushing water filled the air, and the beauty of the landscape surrounded them. The air was sweet with the scent of wildflowers, and the soft rustle of the leaves provided a gentle backdrop to their conversation. Peter walked ahead while Wendy lagged slightly behind, her brow furrowed in thought.

"Wendy, did you see that tree over there? It looks just like a giant's hat!" Peter exclaimed, pointing to a particularly gnarled tree with branches that twisted outward like a wide-brimmed hat. He laughed, twirling in place, his spirit unbroken by the challenges they had faced.

Wendy smiled faintly, but her heart felt heavy. "It's a nice tree, Peter. But... I've been thinking." Peter halted, turning to face her with curiosity.

"Thinking? About what?" Peter asked inquisitively. She hesitated, her gaze drifting to the ground.

"About going home. After we finish this mission." Peter's smile faded, replaced by a look of disbelief.

"Wendy, please! You can't mean it," Peter pleaded, his voice rising above the sound of crashing waves. "You're not really thinking about going home, are you?" Wendy turned to face him, her eyes glistening with unshed tears.

"I miss my mother, Peter. I miss the safety of my home. This place... it's dangerous! We've faced horrors I never imagined—pirates, psycho clowns, and those terrible shadows. I just want to go back to where I belong!" Peter's expression hardened, his jaw clenched.

"But this is where you belong! You're a part of my world, Wendy. You can't just throw that away because you're scared!"

"Scared?" Wendy exclaimed, her

voice trembling with emotion. "It's not just fear, Peter! It's reality! You don't understand the responsibility that comes with being a mother, with caring for others. You refuse to grow up, to face the world, and it's selfish!"

"I swear I will never grow up!" Peter shouted, frustration boiling over. "Growing up means giving up on fun, on adventure! It means leaving behind the magic of Neverland!" Wendy took a deep breath, trying to steady herself.

"But magic isn't everything, Peter! I brought my brothers to this place, and I thought it would be a dream for all of us. But it's been a nightmare! What kind of mother would I be if I let them stay in a place filled with danger and darkness?" Peter stepped closer, desperation in his eyes.

"Once we reach the *Land of the Fairies*, things will change! We'll regain the ability to fly, to truly be free! Just imagine it, Wendy! We can have fun again, just like before!" Wendy shook her head, tears streaming down her cheeks.

"But at what cost, Peter? I can't keep

pretending that this is the life I want. I've always dreamed of being a mother and a *nurse*, of caring for others and making a difference. I can't abandon that dream for the sake of a fantasy!"

Silence hung heavily between them, the sound of the water crashing against the rocks a stark reminder of the tumultuous emotions they faced. Peter looked away, his heart aching at the sight of Wendy's pain.

"I just thought you wanted to be with me, to share this adventure." Wendy's voice softened.

"I do want to be with you, Peter. But I can't sacrifice my future for a life of endless play. Neverland is magical, but it's also a place filled with dangers. I want to create a life where I can nurture, love, and grow—something that this place doesn't offer. Why don't you come home with us? You can stay with us. My parents will take care of you."

"Never!" Peter shouted. "Neverland will always be my home. And I will never grow old." Wendy's face sank and her expression hardened.

"Well then, Peter, it appears we have

both made up our minds."

"We still need to fly in order to get you home, so we must finish the journey."

"Yes, we must," Wendy agreed.

As she turned to walk away, Peter felt a deep sense of loss wash over him. He realized that sometimes, the hardest part of love was letting go. Wendy's longing for home echoed in his heart, a reminder that even in a world of wonder, the heart craved something deeper—connection, safety, and the promise of a future. When they returned to the group, Peter's expression was serious.

"I looked around," he said, his voice steady. "There isn't another way around. We'll have to climb the rock." The group fell silent, the weight of his words sinking in. The reality of the climb ahead loomed large, and uncertainty flickered in their eyes.

"We can do it," Peter continued, trying to instill some confidence. "If we work together, we can make it to the top. We just have to be careful." Wendy glanced at the mountain, then back at her friends.

"It won't be easy, but we have to try," she said, her voice firm.

As they gathered their resolve, the beauty of Neverland around them felt both comforting and daunting, a reminder of what they were fighting for as they prepared to face the challenge ahead.

The group stood at the base of the narrow mountainous rock, a towering silhouette against the bright sky. The sun beat down on them as Peter Pan took the lead, with Michael perched on his back, giggling with excitement.

"This is fun!" Michael exclaimed as if unaware of the danger, his small arms wrapped tightly around Peter's neck.

"Just hold on tight, little buddy!" Peter replied, a grin stretching across his face. The others followed closely behind, their spirits buoyed by the promise of adventure. The initial part of the climb was manageable, with sturdy handholds and a path that wound upward with a gentle incline. Wendy soon captured the lead, encouraging everyone with her cheerful demeanor.

"Look at how far we've come already! We can do this!" Wendy shouted.

"Yeah, but it's not going to last,"

Tootles grumbled, his voice dripping with discontent. "This is way harder than I thought it would be! My arms are already tired!"

"Come on, Tootles! It's just a little climb!" Curly called back, trying to keep the mood light. "If you can't handle it, just think of all the fairy dust we'll get!"

"I'm thinking about how high up we are! What if we fall?" Tootles whined, glancing down at the ground far below.

"You won't fall," Nibs reassured him, though he wasn't entirely sure himself. "Just focus on your grip. We're almost there!"

As they continued their ascent, the rock face grew steeper, the handholds becoming less frequent. The chatter began to fade as the effort required to climb intensified. Tootles was now visibly sweating, his grip faltering.

"I hate climbing! Why did I let you guys drag me into this?"

Just as he voiced his frustration, Tootles lost his grip, his foot slipping on a loose stone. "No! No, no!" he screamed, arms flailing as he felt himself begin to fall.

"TOOTLES!" Wendy shouted, her heart racing.

In a split second, Nibs acted without thinking. He lunged downward, grabbing Tootles by the wrist just as he had let go of the rock.

"I've got you! Hold on!" Nibs strained to pull him back up, his own footing teetering dangerously.

"I can't! I can't hold on!" Tootles cried, panic surging through him.

"Just trust me! We're all here!" Nibs grunted, putting all his strength into the pull. With a final effort, he yanked Tootles back up onto the ledge, both boys collapsing onto the rocky surface, gasping for breath.

"Whew! That was too close!" Curly exclaimed, eyes wide. "You scared us half to death, Tootles!"

"Ugh, I never want to climb again!" Tootles panted, trying to catch his breath.

"Just remember, we're doing this for Tinkerbell and the Fairy Queen!" Peter encouraged, his voice still full of determination. "We can't give up now!"

Slightly nodded with concern and

pride in his eyes. "We're all in this together, Tootles. Just take it one step at a time."

With renewed resolve, they continued their climb, although the ascent had grown increasingly tough. The rocky surface was rough and uneven, and the incline steepened significantly. But with each step, they reminded one another of their purpose, their bond strengthening with every challenge they faced. The top awaited them, and with it, the promise of flying once more.

Chapter 10

Land of the Fairies

As Peter Pan, Wendy, John, Michael, and the remaining Lost Boys finally reached the top of the mountain, the breathtaking view of Neverland sprawled before them, but the beauty of the landscape was quickly overshadowed by a chilling sight. *Captain Hook* stood there, arms crossed, a wicked grin plastered across his face, flanked by his men, all brandishing their swords with menacing intent.

"Well, well, well, if it isn't the Lost Boys and their little leader," Hook sneered, his voice overflowing with mockery. "I must say, I expected a more formidable entrance. You've climbed a mountain just to find your doom."

Peter's pulse raced, and he stepped forward with defiance burning in his eyes. "You won't get away with this, Hook! We're here for Tinkerbell, and you'll pay for what you did to her!"

Hook's grin widened, and a gleam of satisfaction flickered in his eyes.

"Ah, Tinkerbell. Yes, such a spirited little fairy, wasn't she? You know, it was quite exhilarating to finally rid myself of her pesky little presence. Watching the light fade from her eyes was... satisfying," he taunted, his voice dripping with cruelty.

"No!" Michael gasped, tears welling in his eyes. "You're a monster!"

"Indeed, my dear boy, thank you," Hook replied, relishing the anguish he caused. "And it was a beautiful sight, one I'll cherish forever. But enough about her; let's talk about your impending doom!" With a hand gesture from Hook, his men forced them to their knees.

"Let us go!" Wendy exclaimed, anger flaring in her eyes. "You won't win this time, Hook!"

"Oh, but I already have, my dear," Hook chuckled, enjoying their distress. "You see, you've walked right into my trap. I'll take great pleasure in watching you die. Look at you—all of you, kneeling like the pathetic little children you are. It's quite fitting, don't you think?" John clenched his fists, anger bubbling beneath the surface.

"You're a coward, Hook! Attacking us like this? You're nothing but a bully!"

"A bully?" Hook echoed, feigning surprise. "Oh, no, no, my boy. I'm the captain of the *Jolly Roger*, and I have the upper hand. You lot are just a bunch of lost little children, and I'm going to enjoy ending your little adventure here."

"Why do you even want to kill us?" Slightly asked, his voice wavering. "What have we ever done to you?" Hook leaned in closer, his face twisted with malice.

"You've been a thorn in my side for too long. Tinkerbell was just the start. I'll make an example out of all of you! Perhaps I'll let my crew decide the method of your demise—slowly, painfully, or perhaps a quick plunge into the depths of the sea. Choices, choices!"

"No!" Peter shouted, his voice rising above the fear that threatened to consume him. "We won't let you get away with this! You think you can just take everything from us without consequences?"

"Consequences?" Hook chuckled darkly. "The only consequence here is your lives, and those will be extinguished soon enough. You've brought this upon yourselves by meddling in my affairs." Michael picked up a small rock and threw it at Hook, hitting him in the right cheek. "Enough of this!" Hook yelled, his patience thinning. "Take them away! Secure them in the ship! You're all going to be nothing but a pile of bones at the bottom of the sea before the day is done!"

As Peter Pan, Wendy, John, Michael, and the remaining Lost Boys were forcibly dragged away by Captain Hook and his men, the weight of despair settled heavily upon them. Their hearts were racing as they exchanged worried glances. Hook's men laughed cruelly, their swords glinting menacingly in the fading light.

"Keep moving, you little pests," one of Hook's crew growled, shoving Michael forward. "You're going to regret ever crossing the captain!"

But just as the boys felt the heat of hopelessness closing in, a sudden flurry of movement erupted in the air above them. A shimmering cloud of fairies burst forth from the surrounding trees, their delicate wings glinting like jewels in the dimming light. They flew in a frenzy, their tiny forms a whirlwind of color and light, anger radiating from their very being.

"Fairies!" Wendy exclaimed with a look filled with astonishment. "They're here!"

The fairies swooped down with aggressive intensity, their tiny bodies darting and weaving through the air. With a collective shout, they began to attack, launching themselves at Hook and his men with unexpected ferocity. Tiny, glowing orbs of magic burst forth, striking the pirates and causing them to stagger back in shock.

"What in the name of—?!" Hook spluttered, his bravado evaporating as he looked up at the oncoming swarm. "Get them off me!"

The fairies swirled around Hook and his crew, their iridescent wings creating a dazzling spectacle as they unleashed their magic. One particularly bold fairy zoomed straight at Hook, zipping past him and leaving a trail of sparkling dust that caused his hat to fly off his head.

"Retreat!" Hook bellowed, his voice tinged with panic as he stumbled backward. "Get those pests away from me!"

Peter seized the opportunity amidst the chaos. "Now's our chance!" he shouted to the Lost Boys. "Fight back! Grab your knives!"

With a surge of adrenaline, the boys pulled out their small, makeshift knives, their spirits reignited by the sight of the fairies fiercely defending them. Nibs charged at a pirate, swiping at the man's sword with a determined battle cry. "You'll pay for what you did to Tinkerbell!" he yelled, his voice filled with righteous anger.

Tootles, shaking off his earlier fear, lunged forward, catching a pirate off guard and making him stumble. "Take that!" he shouted, newfound confidence surging through him.

Wendy joined the fray, wielding a bunch of sharp rocks as weapons. She threw one, hitting a pirate square in the head and causing him to stumble. Nibs took advantage of the moment and plunged his knife into his stomach.

Amidst the swirling chaos, the fairies' magic illuminated the scene, casting bright flashes of light; and despite the absence of darkness, the bright flashes dazzled and disoriented Hook's men. Curly darted past, tagging a pirate on the shoulder, while Slightly and Michael worked together to fend off another attacker.

"Fight! We can do this!" Peter called, his heart swelling with determination. He danced around the chaos, his movements graceful and precise as he ducked and dodged, taking down a pirate with a swift kick.

But as the battle raged on, Hook, realizing the tide was turning against him, took a step back, his eyes darting around for an escape. "This isn't over!" he shouted, his bluster faltering. "Men, to the woods! We'll regroup and come back for them!"

With that, Captain Hook turned and fled into the dense underbrush, his crew scrambling after him, bewildered and defeated. The fairies' furious onslaught slowed, their energy flickering as they chased Hook and his men into the shadows of the trees.

As the cheers of victory still echoed in the air, a shimmering light began to materialize before Peter Pan. It coalesced into the form of the *Fairy Queen*, her wings sparkling like a cascade of stars. Her expression was urgent, her eyes filled with a both sorrow and determination.

"Peter!" she called, her voice ringing with a melodic urgency. "I need to speak with you!"

"What is it, Your Majesty?" Peter asked, his heart racing as he sensed the gravity of her presence.

"I know about Tinkerbell," she said quickly, her voice trembling with emotion. "Hook killed her."

"How did you know?" Peter asked in confusion.

"I have my sources," she said keenly. "You must chase him! You must finish this once and for all!"

"Oh, I will," Peter said, his voice caught in his throat, anger surging through him like wildfire. "He'll pay for that!"

"Here," the *Fairy Queen* said as she fluttered closer, her wings scattering glimmers of fairy dust that sparkled around

Peter. "This will give you the speed and strength you need." The dust enveloped him, filling him with energy and resolve.

"Thank you!" Peter exclaimed, his spirit ignited by her magic. With a powerful leap, he took to the air, soaring into the woods in pursuit of Hook. The trees blurred beneath him as he darted through the branches, fueled by his tenacious spirit.

"Hook!" Peter shouted, his voice cutting through the stillness of the forest. "You can't escape me!" In the depths of the woods, Hook had stumbled upon a clearing, panting as he leaned against a tree, his boldness fading.

"You think you can catch me, Pan?" he sneered, trying to regain his composure. "You're just a boy!" Peter landed gracefully in front of him, knives glinting in his hands.

"I might be a boy, but I'm not just any boy. You've taken everything from me, and now you'll pay!" With a roar, Hook drew his sword, the blade sparkling ominously in the dappled sunlight.

"Come then, let's see what you've got!"

The two clashed, steel meeting steel

as Peter lunged forward with his two knives, his movements quick and agile. Hook swung his sword fiercely, but Peter danced around him, using his speed to evade the strikes.

"You'll never win, Hook!" he taunted, darting in and out, slashing with his knives.

"Don't be so sure!" Hook growled, desperation creeping into his voice as he swung wildly, trying to corner Peter. "I've bested you before!" But Peter's heart surged with the memory of Tinkerbell, her laughter, her light. Each strike fueled his determination.

"Not this time!" he shouted, dodging another swing and countering with a swift kick that sent Hook stumbling back.

As the fight escalated, the forest felt alive with their struggle, the atmosphere brimming with tension. Peter felt the rush of the fairy dust coursing through him, enhancing his strength and agility. He focused on Hook, who was now panting heavily, his sword faltering.

With a final surge of energy, Peter lunged forward, knives poised. He feinted left, and as Hook instinctively followed, Peter struck right, plunging one of his knives deep into Hook's side.

Hook's eyes widened in shock, the sword slipping from his grasp as he staggered back, clutching the wound.

"No... this can't be..." he gasped with disbelief and fury in his voice.

"Goodbye, Hook," Peter said firmly, watching as the infamous pirate fell to the ground, defeated, his once fearsome presence now diminished.

Just then, the sounds of hurried footsteps echoed through the trees. Wendy, John, Michael, and the Lost Boys burst into the clearing, staring in disbelief at the sight before them.

"Peter!" Wendy cried, rushing forward, her heart racing as she took in the sight of Hook on the ground. "Did you...?"

"I did it," Peter replied, breathing heavily but filled with a sense of relief. "He won't hurt anyone again."

As Wendy and the others gathered around, the realization of what they had faced settled upon them. They stood there, frozen, staring expressionlessly at Hook and Peter.

Suddenly, the vibrant colors of

Neverland faded, replaced by stark white walls and the sterile scent of antiseptic. Peter awoke in a dim room, the chatter of orderlies and the distant cries of patients permeating the air. He was no longer the boy who refused to grow up; he was a man in his twenties, trapped in a mental institution. Confusion gripped his mind as fragments of memory coalesced into a horrifying realization.

The room was a surreal reflection of Neverland. His nametag, attached to his shirt, displayed the name "Peter Panera." The other patients, each in his mind's eye embodying the Lost Boys, stood gawking at him. But it was *Captain Hook* who presided over this nightmarish version of Neverland, donning the guise of the institution's head nurse, his presence commanding and sinister.

As Peter attempted to piece together the fragments of his reality, he noticed a warm, crimson liquid seeping into the fabric of his clothes. Panic surged through him as he looked down to find his hands covered in blood. At his feet lay a nurse with a nametag that read, *"James Bartholomew,"* that resembled Captain Hook. So much so, that it could be his doppelganger. In that moment, the door burst open, and a nurse stumbled in, her gaze filled with terror.

"Peter, what did you do?" she screamed, her voice a piercing siren in the oppressive silence that followed.

Peter's chest throbbed, the lines between fantasy and reality blurring into a nightmare from which he could not awaken. The echoes of Neverland haunted him, and as he stood over the body of what he believed to be his greatest foe, he realized that perhaps he had never truly escaped the darkness—he was merely trapped in a different kind of madness. The world around him spun into chaos, and all that remained was the chilling laughter of a boy who never grew up, now forever lost in the shadows of his own creation.

As Peter stood frozen in the plain, white room, the nurse's frantic cries echoed around him. Time seemed to distort, stretching infinitely as he grappled with the horrific scene unfolding before his eyes. The blood, warm and thick, pooled around Jame's body, and the realization of what he had done sent waves of nausea crashing over him.

"Peter! Focus!" the nurse shouted, her voice slicing through the fog of confusion. She rushed to his side, her hands trembling as she reached for him. "You need to calm down! I can help you!"

But help? What did that mean now? Peter's thoughts spiraled back to Neverland—the vibrant island that had promised eternal youth and adventure. He remembered the thrill of flight, the joy of laughter, and the camaraderie of the Lost Boys. Yet, intertwined with those memories were shadows of fear, betrayal, and bloodshed.

His mind raced back to his last conversation with Wendy, when she said she wanted to go home; she wanted to have kids and grow up. Had he truly saved her, or had he condemned her to a fate worse than death. The guilt gnawed at him, a festering wound in his heart.

Suddenly, the room felt suffocating. The walls, once merely plain, took on a menacing quality, closing in around him. The other patients who had once appeared as mere reflections of his childhood characters now stared at him with a mixture of pity and fear. They were trapped in their own nightmares, but Peter felt the heaviness of theirs pressing against him.

The nurse, her nametag reading, "Wendy," was now kneeling beside James' body, looked back at Peter, her expression shifting from shock to something resembling understanding.

"Peter, you're not alone in this. We all have our demons. Just talk to me—tell me what happened."

As her words settled, visions of Neverland surged back, like waves crashing against the shore of his consciousness. He recounted the tale in fragmented bursts, Hook murdering Tinkerbell, their adventure west, and the final confrontation. Each word pulled him deeper into the abyss, the weight of his actions pulling him down like an anchor.

"I didn't want to hurt anyone," Peter pleaded, desperation lacing his voice. "I thought I could save her. I thought... I thought I was still a hero." The nurse's eyes softened, but the fear remained.

"You need to face what you've done, Peter. This isn't just in your head. It's real, and it has consequences."

As he listened to her, a creeping realization settled in, he was no longer the carefree boy who could escape the consequences of his actions. The line between right and wrong had blurred, and the harsh truth was that he was lost in a nightmare of his own making.

Just as he began to comprehend the enormity of his situation, the door burst open once more. A group of orderlies entered, their expressions grave as they assessed the scene. They moved swiftly, their presence both intimidating and authoritative. Peter felt a surge of instinctual fear; he was no longer in control of his own fate.

"Get him out of here!" one of the orderlies barked, and before Peter could react, they seized him, dragging him away from the chaos of the room. The nurse reached out, her voice rising in protest, but it was drowned out by Peter's own panic.

"Wait! No! I didn't mean to! I didn't want this!" he shouted, thrashing against their grips as they pulled him down the sterile hallway. The fluorescent lights flickered above, casting shadows that danced along the walls.

As they restrained him, memories of Neverland flooded his mind—the laughter, the adventures, and the friendships, all tainted by the dark turn of events. Was he truly the villain of this story, or merely a misunderstood boy caught in a world that had spiraled out of control?

The orderlies led him to a small, stark room, devoid of color and warmth. They forced him inside and locked the door, leaving him alone with his thoughts. He sank to the floor, the reality of his situation crashing down around him like waves in a storm. In the silence, whispers began to echo in his mind—voices from the past, from the Lost Boys, from Wendy, and even from Hook. Each one tugged at the frayed edges of his sanity, demanding to be heard.

"You're not a boy anymore, Peter," one voice whispered. "You're just a broken man running from his demons."

Peter curled up against the wall, tears streaming down his face as he realized that the battle was far from over. The shadows of Neverland loomed large, and as the specter of Captain Hook lingered in his mind, he knew he would have to confront the darkness within himself. The true horror of Neverland was not the pirates or the monsters; it was the reckoning that awaited him—the confrontation with the boy who refused to grow up and the man he had become. As the shadows danced in the corners of the room, Peter understood that his journey was just beginning, and the nightmare was only a reflection of the battle for his soul.

Chapter 11

One Week Later

The late afternoon sun filtered through the blinds of Dr. Eleanor Hart's office, casting striped shadows across the walls. The room was palpable with unease, a reflection of the turmoil following the incident involving *Peter Panera*.

Dr. Hart sat at her desk, her hands folded, keenly focused on Dr. Mark Sullivan, who leaned forward, a notepad resting in his lap.

"How is James doing?" Dr. Sullivan asked, his tone measured, betraying his concern. Dr. Hart sighed, glancing out the window momentarily before meeting his gaze.

"He's still in critical condition but showing signs of improvement. They've managed to stabilize him, yet it's going to be a long road. He's fighting, but it's touch and go." Dr. Sullivan nodded, absorbing the gravity of her words.

"Has James ever mentioned how he lost his hand? I can't imagine what he must have gone through." Dr. Hart sighed, running a hand through her hair, the weight of their conversation heavy in the air.

"He told me it was a bad car accident... he swerved to avoid a deer, flipped the car, and... well, he didn't make it out unscathed. It's been a rough road for him." Dr. Sullivan frowned, his heart aching for the man.

"That's just terrible. And now, to be attacked at work by a patient? It's like he can't catch a break."

"Exactly," Dr. Hart nodded, her voice thick with empathy. "He's been through so much already, and now this. It's heartbreaking to see someone so kind and dedicated face such adversity."

Dr. Sullivan sat down and leaned back in his chair, concern etched on his face as he turned to Dr. Hart.

"I had a chance to speak with Peter a couple of days ago. He believes he's Peter Pan—says he can fly, and he's here to save Wendy."

"Save Wendy?" Dr. Hart responds. "Nurse Wendy?" Dr. Hart's brow furrowed in confusion. "From what exactly?"

"From Captain Hook," Dr. Sullivan replied, his voice steady. "He's convinced that James is Hook, and that Nurse Wendy is in grave danger because of him." Dr. Hart leaned back in her chair, her expression an amalgamation of disbelief and concern.

"So, in his mind, him wounding James was an act of heroism?"

"Exactly. He told me that Wendy was in peril here and that he had to intervene. He believes Hook traveled here from *Neverland* to kill her to get back at him, and he believes that he was saving her life," Dr. Sullivan explained, rubbing his temples as if the weight of Peter's delusions was pressing down on him.

"Does he have any grasp on reality?"

Dr. Hart asked, her frustration simmering just below the surface. Dr. Sullivan shook his head slowly.

"Not really. He is deeply entrenched in this fantasy. He described Neverland in vivid detail—flying, adventures, and battles against villains. To him, it's all very real." Dr. Hart crossed her arms, contemplating the implications.

"And what about Wendy? How does she fit into this narrative?"

"To Peter, she's the innocent character in danger," Dr. Sullivan said. "Peter says that he took Wendy to Neverland, and after an adventure to see the *Fairy Queen*, Wendy returned home, grew up, and became a nurse. He believes she's being targeted by Hook to get back at him, and he genuinely believes he's here to protect her." Dr. Hart frowned.

"Does Wendy know any of this?" Dr. Hart asked.

"No, no," Dr. Sullivan replied. "Peter explained that he kept it from her to protect her."

"Did he mention why she did not recognize him?" Dr. Hart asked.

"He said that they hadn't seen each other in years, since they were very young."

"This is more than just a delusion; it's a complete recontextualization of his reality," Dr. Hart said, baffled. "We can't overlook how dangerous this can be, especially if he feels justified in his actions." Dr. Sullivan took a deep breath, shifting in his seat.

"I plan to continue my sessions with him. We need to find a way to gently unravel this narrative without dismissing it outright. If we can understand the root of these beliefs, we might guide him back to reality." Dr. Hart leaned forward, her expression serious.

"We need to approach this very carefully. The line between his fantasy world and our reality is razor-thin. If he feels threatened, he could lash out again, thinking he's still in that heroic role."

"Trust me, I'm aware of the risks," Dr. Sullivan affirmed, his eyes steady. "But Peter deserves a chance to heal. We owe it to him—and to James—to help him navigate this." A heavy silence filled the space as both doctors contemplated the complexity of the situation. Finally, Dr. Hart spoke, her voice softer.

"Let's make sure we have a safety plan in place. I don't want to see another incident like this happen again."

"Agreed," Dr. Sullivan replied, a firmness in his tone. "We'll work together to find a way to reach him. There's hope, even in the darkest of fantasies."

As they continued their discussion, the shadows in the room deepened, mirroring the challenges that lay ahead. They were determined to help Peter find his way back, but the path would be fraught with obstacles, both real and imagined. The muted light of Dr. Eleanor Hart's office cast a contemplative glow on the scattered papers and medical reports strewn across her desk. Dr. Sullivan leaned back in his chair, the weight of their recent discussions still lingering in the air.

A few doors down, an orderly was in James' quarters going through his belongings to gather some clothes for him to take them to the hospital and found something... unusual. As the orderly rummaged through the cluttered shelves, he stumbled upon a hidden compartment cleverly disguised behind a loose panel. With anticipation, he pried it open to reveal a tarnished hook, its jagged edges catching the faint light in a way that sent a chill down his spine. Beside it lay an amulet, intricately engraved with symbols that seemed to pulse with an ancient power. The orderly's mind raced with the chilling stories Peter Pan had recounted—the tales of Captain Hook, a vengeful spirit who had crossed realms to seek retribution against Wendy.

Peter had spoken of the infamous hook as well as a lucky amulet that the captain carried around with him. Could it be that James, in some twist of fate, had traveled from Neverland, harboring dark intentions toward the girl who had captivated Peter's heart?

Yet, as he held the relics in his trembling hands, doubt began to cloud his thoughts. James had always seemed like a man haunted by his past, a tortured soul rather than a villainous figure. Were these items truly tokens of his identity as Hook, or merely remnants of a childhood obsession, misplaced artifacts that had no bearing on his present? The orderly felt the weight of uncertainty pressing down on him, grappling with the possibility that James might embody the very essence of evil described by Peter, or that he was simply a man ensnared in a web of coincidences. In this moment of ambiguity, the line between hero and monster blurred, leaving the orderly questioning the true nature of James and the sinister legacy of *Captain Hook*.

The End

Make sure that you check out Will's latest literary triumphs…

"The Embittered of Oz"
"The Curse of Nanny Wilkins"
"The Horrors of Willville: Paranormal Edition"

All ON SALE NOW!!!

Please visit:

https://willsavive.com/

Facebook:

https://www.facebook.com/WillSavive

www.ingramcontent.com/pod-product-compliance
Lightning Source LLC
Chambersburg PA
CBHW022126170626
46808CB00002B/860